When Darius took her into his arms, she went gladly.

When she heard his groan of satisfaction, she felt her heart kick into overdrive.

"I've known you fifteen years . . . twenty maybe," Cyg burbled, her fingers tracing his jawline, watching a muscle jump in his neck.

"One hundred last Wednesday," Darius muttered. "This is crazy. I stopped necking years ago."

"Fun, huh?" Cyg gripped his hair between her hands with a gentle fierceness.

"You make me feel as if I'm full of helium," Darius groaned. "Weird." He brushed some leaves from her dungarees, then lifted her into the saddle. "With you now I feel like I'm reliving every Christmas and every birthday of my life." His upturned face was flushed as he stood next to her saddle, his hands still at her waist. "Stupid, isn't it?"

"No." Cyg leaned down and touched his chin. "Lovely."

WHAT ARE *LOVESWEPT* ROMANCES?

They are stories of true romance and touching emotion. We believe those two very important ingredients are constants in our highly sensual and very believable stories in the *LOVESWEPT* line. Our goal is to give you, the reader, stories of consistently high quality that may sometimes make you laugh, sometimes make you cry, but are always fresh and creative and contain many delightful surprises within their pages.

Most romance fans read an enormous number of books. Those they truly love, they keep. Others may be traded with friends and soon forgotten. We hope that each *LOVESWEPT* romance will be a treasure—a "keeper." We will always try to publish

*LOVE STORIES YOU'LL NEVER FORGET
BY AUTHORS YOU'LL ALWAYS REMEMBER*

The Editors

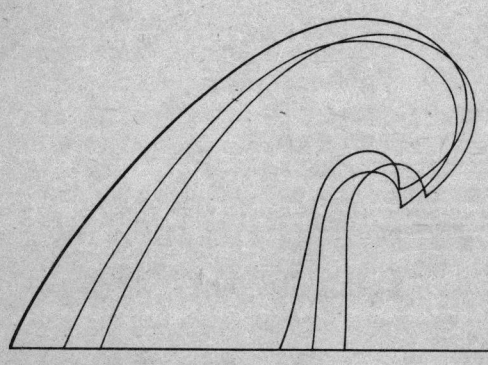

LOVESWEPT • 15
Helen Mittermeyer
Brief Delight

BANTAM BOOKS • TORONTO • NEW YORK • LONDON • SYDNEY

BRIEF DELIGHT
A Bantam Book / August 1983

Two lines from "Never Give all the Heart" by W. B. Yeats from IN THE SEVEN WOODS. By permission of A. P. Watt Ltd.

LOVESWEPT and the wave device are trademarks of Bantam Books, Inc.

All rights reserved.
Copyright © 1983 by Helen Mittermeyer.
Cover art copyright © 1983 by Ray Kursar.
This book may not be reproduced in whole or in part, by mimeograph or any other means, without permission.
For information address: Bantam Books, Inc.

ISBN 0-553-21614-7

Published simultaneously in the United States and Canada

Bantam Books are published by Bantam Books, Inc. Its trademark, consisting of the words "Bantam Books" and the portrayal of a rooster, is Registered in U.S. Patent and Trademark Office and in other countries. Marca Registrada. Bantam Books, Inc., 666 Fifth Avenue, New York, New York 10103.

PRINTED IN THE UNITED STATES OF AMERICA

O   0 9 8 7 6 5 4 3 2 1

One

She, Cyg Melton, sometime model and part-time physiotherapist, could hardly unclench her teeth as the limousine pulled up the winding drive to the cement and brick pile that was Phil Tabor's residence on Long Island. "I'm sorry I came," she muttered to her roommate Kim Jones who just shrugged.

"Where were you going to get the money to pay Mrs. Tonetti the back rent? And don't forget you were able to give her a little for next month's, too. Have you forgotten how scarce modeling jobs have been for us lately?"

"I haven't forgotten," Cyg mumbled.

She was just skinning by on the small salary she made working two evenings a week at the Apollo Health Club. Her lack of money had made Kim's latest proposal about Phil's parties seem more attractive. Days of plain peanut butter sandwiches washed down with Big Apple tap water had made her almost faint as Kim described the food served at other parties at Phil's house. "This is crazy," Cyg had mumbled that day while they ate their "rations."

"I know you don't like Phil, Cyg, but he does give great parties and I don't think I would have met nearly as many important people if it hadn't been for Phil introducing them to me," Kim had said, wrinkling up her nose at the peanut butter.

"You haven't had many more modeling jobs than I have, Kim. So don't heap too many laurels on Mr. Tabor's head," Cyg pointed out drily.

"You just don't understand these things." Then her face cleared. "Oh, Cyg, if you could see the *miles* of shrimp and lobster on the buffet tables at Phil's place and the breads . . . and the hot foods. They had bouillabaisse last time. You know how you love . . ."

"Stop!" Cyg held up her hand, palm outward. "I can't stand to hear anymore. Oh, my Lord, listen to my stomach rumble."

Kim kept after her for three more days, but it wasn't until Mrs. Tonetti said they might have to move if they didn't pay their rent on time that Cyg conceded. She would go to the party as a model, a paid hostess though she knew the whole idea was pretty shady. But she would insist on getting that three hundred dollars in advance so she could pay her landlady. She didn't like Phil, but his money made it possible for her to pay Mrs. Tonetti the balance on last month's rent and something for the coming month.

Now, as she watched the wooden-faced attendant open the door of the limousine for them, she wished she was back in her third-floor walk-up with her peanut butter sandwich and glass of water. She just *had* to stop feeling embarrassed and ashamed for being a paid party girl; she needed the money. That was all there was to it. And, besides, she wasn't going to do anything wrong. It wasn't like she was selling *herself*.

"Honestly Cyg, you kill me," Kim hissed, looking her friend over from top to toe. "Here you are at this gorgeous house; we're going to have great food and lots of fun and you look like you're going to a funeral." She clucked in a disgusted way.

"Why did you have to wear that blouse and skirt? Why didn't you wear the satin pants and blouse?"

"Suede is fine. This is the best outfit I own and I like it on me." Cyg looked straight at her friend. "I wish I hadn't come."

Kim glared at her. "For heaven's sake don't . . ."

Neither of them saw Phil Tabor until he put an arm around each of them. "Hi, girls, come on in." He kissed Kim full on the mouth. When he turned toward Cyg, she gave him a cold look and backed away.

"Ah, yes, the Queen of the Swans, the oh, so cool Cygnet Melton." Phil smiled, but Cyg could tell he was irritated with her.

She trailed behind Phil and Kim, taking deep breaths to steady her nerves.

The foyer of the house was huge, a crystal chandelier suspended from the two-story-high round ceiling lighting it brilliantly. People milled around there before moving into what Philip described as the drawing room on one side of the hall or the library on the other.

Cyg trailed Kim and Philip into the drawing room. A fixed smile on her face, she acknowledged introductions and promptly forgot the names. A prickly feeling of being watched made her turn. Her first thought was that those green eyes couldn't possibly be that emerald color! She swallowed and made a real effort to look away. But even when her gaze slid away, she could still see the man's craggy face, his deep chestnut-colored hair with the reddish highlights.

"Hello." The voice had a rich timbre to it, a warmth.

Cyg took a deep breath before she turned, her modeling training forcing her body to relax. "Hello." She put out her hand and felt it taken by a much larger one than hers, the fingers long and strong. He was so tall, with the broad-shouldered build of an athlete.

"I'm Darius Chadwick." He didn't release her hand, instead he maneuvered her closer to him and away from the others. "Let me get you something to drink." His voice had a sensual harshness.

"I'd like a Perrier . . . ah . . . a white wine would be fine, thank you." Kim had told her to have wine and not seltzer water. Cyg decided she would nurse the wine and seize the first chance to get some seltzer water. The hell with Kim.

Darius Chadwick signaled to a waiter. The drinks seemed to appear like magic.

"Now are you going to tell me your name?" Darius asked, somehow managing to steer them to a space near wide french windows that were open to catch the rays of the late afternoon sun. His palm was warm on her back.

"Cygnet Melton." Cyg shivered in the breeze coming through the doors, unable to look away from those hot green eyes.

Darius's eyes narrowed on her, then he set down his glass and removed his soft suede sport coat. "Since my jacket is almost the same tan color as your skirt, it should be all right." He placed the jacket around her shoulders, holding it closed with his two hands under her chin. "Of course, it's too big for you. You're tall but too slender." He bent down and kissed her nose. "Whoever named you Baby Swan?" One hand feathered up from her hip to the side of her breast.

Cyg gulped, closing her eyes at the sudden dizziness when his lips made slow forays across her cheekbones. She stepped back. "Most people don't even make the connection that a cygnet is a baby swan."

"I'm an animal lover," Darius whispered, chuckling.

"Oh." Cyg sloshed a little of her wine on her hand. Gritting her teeth, she tried to force the trembling in her limbs to stop as she wiped at the spill. "I'm . . . I'm sorry. I've spilled some wine on your sport coat."

Darius was bent over, his body screening them from the others in the room. "No problem," he muttered, his hand rising to cup her chin. "Your eyes and your hair are the same honey color. Beautiful. Tell me about yourself."

"Not much to tell." Cyg felt giddy from looking into his eyes. "I model when I get the work and I have a job in a health club, too."

"Do you like parties?" Darius's dark chestnut eyebrows drew together like a bridge across his nose, his gaze sharpening on her, a sensual hardness there.

"Some I like . . . some I don't."

"Phil fancies himself an entrepreneur of entertainment." Darius lifted her hand to his mouth. "Pretty hand. No rings."

"No." Cyg smiled, thinking she would have told anyone else who treated her this way to get lost. "I haven't tried an engagement or marriage yet. Are you? Married, I mean?"

"I was. Divorced. No children. Reasonably healthy, reasonably wealthy—"

"And, of course, wise," Cyg interrupted, laughing, liking the answering gleam of laughter in those green eyes.

"Of course. Didn't I know about cygnets being baby swans?" He pressed another kiss into her palm. "Tell me why your parents named you Cygnet."

"Actually they call me Cyg, as most people do." She smiled as she thought of her parents, the happiness they shared with each other on the farm in eastern New York where they raised and trained thoroughbred horses. It wasn't a big operation but Bud and Muriel Melton had made a good living at it and wanted no other kind of life. "It was my Aunt Lena, my father's sister, who suggested the name Cygnet. She said I was all soft and cuddly like a baby swan when I was born."

"Still are," Darius mumbled, his gaze roving on her face, her eyes, her cheeks, her nose, her skin. "Cygnet is definitely the name for you."

She felt as though he was reeling her in, playing her like a game fish. Her breathing was erratic, she was off balance.

And that was just the beginning. He seemed insatiably curious and Cyg could never remember telling anyone the things she told Darius about herself. When she would pause, he would urge her to continue, not seeming to tire of hearing about her life; his eyes held a restless heat that made her tingle.

"So, you trained as a physiotherapist in Duluth, Minnesota? How is it that you aren't working in that field full time?" Darius asked, staring blankly at Phil when he came up to speak to them. Phil soon faded away.

Cyg shrugged. "I couldn't get full-time work. So I came back East and finished my undergraduate work at a liberal arts college. I decided against teaching and came to New York City to work." She tried to smile. "I think I would have had better luck upstate."

"The job market is very tight," Darius agreed. "Maybe I could find a job for you."

"You don't even know me."

"I'm going to know you," Darius promised her, chuckling.

When Kim hurried up to her sometime later, giving Darius a very warm smile, and told her that it was time to dress for dinner, Cyg looked at her watch in surprise. She had been talking to Darius for almost two hours.

"I'll wait for you down here after I've changed," Darius said, stilling her hands when she would have removed his jacket and handed it back to him. "I'll get it another time." He took her chin in his hand. "Don't be too long."

"No." Cyg choked. She turned to follow Kim who chattered all the way up the stairs and to their room. Cyg realized that she had no idea of the way they had come and that she would need directions to find her way back to the drawing room.

The minute the door to their room was closed, Kim was full of questions. "Tell me about the great Darius Chadwick. Phil didn't say he was going to be here this weekend. He's up to those gorgeous green eyes of his in money."

"Ah . . . we just talked." Cyg grabbed her dressing gown and headed for the bathroom, Kim's outraged wails in her ears. For some reason she didn't want to discuss Darius with Kim.

While the shower coursed over her body, Cyg thought of him, then, unbidden, came images of Len Peters whom she had dated while she was in Minnesota. She'd thought she wanted to marry him. Yet in two short hours Darius had had an even greater impact on her than Len had had in all their time together; Cyg had never known the sunburst feeling she was experiencing now with anyone else.

She dried her long hair with the hair dryer, fluffing its natural curl with one hand, while brushing it so that the sides were smooth and the back fell in a cascade of curls. She stared into the mirror at her light hazel eyes, recalling what Darius said about her hair and eyes: "Beautiful. Honey colored."

She slipped on flesh-colored bikini briefs and bra, then wrapped a short terry cloth robe around her, and braced herself to go into the bedroom to see the clothes that Philip was supplying for both girls for the evening. "If it isn't my style, I won't wear it." Cyg nodded firmly at her image in the mirror before yanking open the door.

She yelped at the cloth of gold silk that Kim held out to her. "It can't weigh three ounces," she said, astonished as she took the garment in hand. "It's indecent," she muttered.

"Don't be like that." Kim snorted, disgusted. "How can you tell until you try it on?"

"I can tell." Cyg turned away from her roommate. "I'll put it on, but if I don't like it . . . off it comes." She punctuated her words with a jabbing finger.

Cyg removed the robe and her bra. The dress slithered down her body and clung to her like a magnet. She turned toward the mirror and gasped. "Lord, it looks as though I've slipped into a layer of gold skin."

"You look gorgeous." There was reluctant envy in Kim's voice. "Your hair looks like curly wheat, and your eyes look almost the same color as the dress . . . and your skin . . ." Kim paused. "Phil must have been paying a lot more attention to you than I realized."

Cyg blinked, looking away from her own image and toward the image of Kim, whose brunette beauty was enhanced by a deep purple dress. "Don't be silly. Phil never looks at anyone but you—and you know you look great in that color."

Kim smiled, her good humor restored. She stepped next to Cyg, lifting her hair from her neck with one hand. "Yes, we both look good don't we? Lord, Cyg, you're almost skinny, but you have the loveliest curves." Kim shrugged, and took Cyg's arm. "Come on, we've been up here long enough."

When they descended the stairs together, there was a growing murmur as more and more masculine heads turned their way.

Cyg braced herself, calling on all her model's training to give her the poise she needed. She tried not to look for the chestnut hair with the reddish highlights.

When a man reached out to take her hand as

she and Kim reached the bottom of the stairs, she turned eagerly. It wasn't Darius.

"Hello, sweetie. I'm claiming you for—"

"Have you been waiting long, darling?" Darius was there, lifting her hand free of the other man's grasp, giving him a cold stare before gazing at Cyg again, his look turning hot and too . . . possessive.

"No." She felt breathless. She took deep gulps of air, then was embarrassed when she saw the way Darius watched the rise and fall of her breasts.

"Damn, I don't want anyone else looking at you in that dress," he muttered, putting an arm around her waist and edging her away from the others.

Somehow he managed to get them drinks, then with unspoken consent they found a quiet spot in the solarium. The last of the day blossomed in myriad colors in the lavender, burnt-orange sky, then slowly faded into pale purple twilight.

"Did you arrange that?" Cyg whispered after they had watched for a long silent time.

"Yes," Darius whispered back. "I wanted something that would come a little close to the way I'm feeling right now . . . and to the way you're looking. Out of this world."

Cyg swallowed and turned to look full into his face. "You do have a way with words." She felt his expert loveplay like a cobweb she had walked into.

"I'm feeling lyrical." Darius gave her a lopsided grin that made his craggy face look boyish for a moment. "And since I've been told that I have a tin ear when it comes to music . . ." He shrugged, his slow smile widening when he heard her laugh.

"Are you telling me you're tone deaf?" Cyg didn't believe him.

"Well, maybe not totally, but I'm generally asked to sing in a lower tone at songfests."

"Songfests? And have you been to many?" Cyg felt happiness bubble in her at the way he watched her every move, smothering the voice of caution deep inside.

"Of course. At college, among my family—very large incidentally. I'm sure you'd find them boring, but back to singing. Sometimes I get together with friends and we sing the old fraternity songs—"

"Dirty ditties, no doubt." Cyg laughed, not remembering when she had felt so carefee. She took a long sip of her white wine and managed not to shiver. She blinked a few times to clear the fuzzy feeling she was getting.

"Do you sing?" Darius asked, signaling to an attendant for another glass of wine for her.

Cyg saluted him with her glass and took another sip of wine. The second glass definitely tasted better than the first. "I sang in the church choir at home and I studied piano and voice in school." She took a deep breath and looked up at him, wishing she could watch him forever. "I even sang in a musical in college." She giggled, surprising herself. She had never been a giggler. "It was the classic success story." She hiccuped, put her hand up to her mouth and mumbled, "Sorry. At first I helped with sewing the costumes, then the understudy to the lead singer came down with a flu bug." Cyg took another sip of wine and waggled her finger at him. "Our dorm used to get a great deal of twenty-four-hour bug . . . bugs? Why are you laughing? You're not listening to my story." Cyg hauled in a deep shuddering breath.

"Yes, I am." Darius leaned down to kiss the end of her nose. "Thank you for being here today. I never expected anyone like you."

"You're welcome." Cyg frowned. "Now I've forgotten what I was saying . . . and it was very important."

"The understudy became—"

"Right." Cyg snapped her fingers. "Thank you. Ahem. Yes. Well, they asked me to understudy because I was the only one in the stage crew that could read music." Cyg flung out her arm. "The rest is history."

"You were a star."

"Well, no. They couldn't hear me that well in the back of the auditorium, but . . ." Cyg flung up one hand and accepted another glass of wine with the other. The third glass was far superior to the other two. ". . . I didn't forget the lyrics of any of the songs. Not bad, huh?"

"Great." Darius chuckled, taking the glass from her hand. "Now, I think I had better get you some dinner."

"Good," Cyg said gratefully. "You know I ate the rest of the fruit in the bowl in our room." She frowned. "Kim ate all the bananas . . . I like bananas." She yawned. "Oh, dear, pardon me. It's not that I'm tried. It's just that I haven't eaten anything but the fruit all day and when I'm hungry, I yawn." She smiled at Darius who was frowning now.

"You're too damn skinny. Come on, we're going to eat." He put his arm around her and steered her through the drawing room to a large dining room behind it, double doors standing open to the drawing room.

"Ohhh." Cyg felt her eyes widen as she took in the array of food on the long table and side buffets. "Kim said there was a *mile* of shrimp here the last time she came. That's why I agreed to come with her," Cyg said in a low voice to Darius.

"I'm glad something brought you," he murmured into her skin as he bent to kiss her cheek. "It's like getting a special prize in a Christmas stocking." He shook his head. "I never imagined I'd meet anyone like you at one of Phil's parties."

Cyg's mouth watered as she watched Darius briskly instruct the waiter on which foods to serve and directed him to bring their plates to them in the solarium. She looked over her shoulder to watch the man fill the plates as Darius began to lead her away. "What if he forgets the shrimp?" Cyg squeaked.

"He won't forget." Darius chuckled, his arm tightening at her waist, one hand kneading her flesh, his fingers making the hair on her body lift.

"Are you sure? I thought he had very shifty eyes." Cyg dragged her heels.

"I'll go back for more if he doesn't put enough on your plate," Darius assured her.

"You're a good man." Cyg leaned on him.

"Thank you."

"You're welcome." Cyg jerked erect. "What if they run out before you get back a second time?"

"They won't." He showed her to a table for two that another waiter gestured to them to take. "Ah, here comes our man now . . . and I don't think he's forgotten anything."

Though Cyg felt a little woozy, it didn't interfere with her appetite. In fact she felt considerably better the more she ate.

"You are slender, but you have a marvelous appetite," Darius said in approval as Cyg munched on her second roll.

"I was hungry." She reddened.

"I know," he said gently. "I wasn't criticizing you. I loved watching you eat . . . and eating with you."

She smiled at him. She could not remember being so relaxed, having such an overwhelming feeling of well-being.

After some luscious pastries and coffee, Phil came over to the table with two brandy snifters. "I insist you try this, Darius. My uncle buys this in France, has it bottled just for the family."

Cyg wanted to refuse, but under Phil's mocking look, she accepted the snifter and sipped the warm, amber-colored liquid. It was not unpalatable to her, but she realized that the wine had been more than enough for her. By the time the music began for dancing in the solarium, Cyg was definitely feeling lightheaded.

"Dance with me?" Darius asked, watching her closely.

"Yes, I love to dance." Cyg made a conscious effort not to weave as she walked ahead of Darius into the center of the room.

Held close in his arms, she delighted in twining her arms around his neck. They swayed to the dreamy tempo of a love ballad the musicians were playing. She hadn't realized she had begun to sing until Darius whispered in her ear.

"I love it when you sing to me." The husky timbre of his voice accelerated her pulse. She tightened her arms around his neck. His body was like a sensual shroud to hers.

Cyg had no idea of time as they danced one dance after the other. When they stopped for a moment at the edge of the dance floor, Darius asked her if she was thirsty. She nodded, smiling at him.

"Excuse me. I don't see a waiter. I'll be right back." He let his mouth touch hers for just a second. "Don't move."

"I won't." But she did; she took a deep breath and moved to a chair placed near a potted palm. She sank onto it and didn't see Phil until he was right in front of her.

"All alone, Cyg? Let's dance." Phil reached down to take her hand.

She pulled her hand back. "I'm waiting for Darius." She blinked at him twice, finding it hard to focus.

"Disappear, Phil." Darius spoke softly behind Tabor. "Here's your wine, Cygnet. Do remember I'm your guest, Phil."

Phil uttered a harsh laugh and walked away, his back stiff.

Cyg sipped the wine, wishing she had told Darius to get her seltzer water. Her mouth stayed dry even when she finished the wine. She yawned three times.

"This time it isn't because you're hungry." Darius took the glass from her, a rueful smile on his face. "And I thought the night was just beginning."

"I don't think I mentioned," Cyg began in measured tones as she rose, "that alcohol doesn't agree with me. It makes me sleepy." She felt her eyes flutter shut as she stood there in front of him.

She opened her eyes a short time later as he steered her out of the room. Darius swept her into his arms and carried her up the stairs to the room she shared with Kim and deposited her on the bed. "Thank you." She closed her eyes again.

"Good night, Cygnet."

She thought she felt him kiss her, but the blackness of sleep took her so fast she wasn't sure.

Her dreams were of a tall, broad-shouldered man who could have starred in any movie or TV show, whose smile was a passionate slash in a sensual face that heated her even in the dream.

She called out to him as he began to fade, his laughter like a Pied Piper's tune pulling her to him. She had never run so fast but still she couldn't catch him.

Two

Cyg woke the next morning with a pain between her eyes that made her think her skull was being devoured by wild beasts. She noticed that Kim was not in the other bed.

She jerked to a sitting position when she saw the silver basket of violets sitting on the night table. She had to blink twice to focus and read the card attached to the flowers.

WOULD YOU LIKE TO GO RIDING? PLAY TENNIS? DO NOTHING? OPEN YOUR DOOR AND THERE I'LL BE. LOVE, DARIUS.

Cyg eased out of bed, only moaning once, and went to the door, not really believing Darius *would* be there. She opened it a crack.

"Hi." He waggled his fingers at her. "I have coffee and juice. Interested?" His eyes went over her like a sexy CAT scan.

"Yes." She swallowed hard, her throat desert dry. She reached for the tray that Darius had lifted from the floor, but he shook his head and walked past her into the room, putting the tray on a low table near the window.

"How . . ." Cyg licked her lips and tried again. "How did you know when I would wake up?"

"I just told the butler to bring me fresh pots of

coffee every twenty minutes." He smiled at her surprised expression, handing her steaming coffee in a delicate porcelain cup.

She sipped the scalding liquid until the cup was empty. "Could I have the orange juice now? Black coffee leaves a bad taste in my mouth."

Darius shouted with laughter, making her wince. "Why didn't you tell me to add milk?"

Cyg yawned and waved her hand. "Too much trouble," she mumbled, making her way to the bathroom, the juice glass clutched in one hand.

"Does this mean we'll be doing nothing today?" Amusement laced his voice. "That might be more interesting."

Cyg stopped in front of the bathroom door, not turning to look at him. "No." She inhaled, putting the ice cold juice glass up to her forehead and holding it there. "I like riding, but first I need a long shower . . ." She stopped dead and looked down at the flesh-colored silk nightie she was wearing. She couldn't remember putting it on last night.

"I put it on for you," Darius whispered from across the room.

"Oh." Cyg could feel her face getting warm. She walked into the bathroom and shut the door firmly behind her.

She let the steamy shower soak into her, not even bothering to lather her body or her hair. The very hot water was like a soft massage, wiping away the aches of her body.

She was beginning to wonder if she would ever get up the strength to soap herself when she felt a draft as the shower door was opened.

"How did I know that you would be just standing here and not washing?" Darius laughed, but there was no laughter in the eyes that traveled from her foot to forehead and back.

"Are . . . are you coming . . . into the shower?" she asked timidly.

"No, because if I did, we'd go right back to your bed . . . and you did say that you wanted to go riding, didn't you?"

"I want to go riding," Cyg said woodenly.

"But I *am* going to wash you to hurry you along. Okay?" He began rolling up his sleeves.

"No," Cyg croaked. "I . . . I can do it. Be out in five minutes." She turned her back on him to face the shower head.

"Ummm. Beautiful," Darius said, then patted her derriere gently.

Cyg sensed the shower door had closed. She sagged against the tiled wall, feeling as though she had just finished third in the Boston Marathon. It took her long seconds to get her breath back. She would have let him! She would have let him wash her, then make love to her!

She scrubbed her head and her body with a ferocity that made her flinch a few times but it seemed to get her blood going and let her forget how weakly she would have submitted to Darius Chadwick if he had crooked his finger. "Fool. Fool. Fool," she grated to herself. "Some independent lady you are."

She continued to berate herself as she reached for a bath sheet hanging on warming rods on the wall. While she was still swathed in the bath sheet and drying her hair, the door opened again.

"Can I help?" Darius's eyes were a hot green liquid.

"Ah . . . I'm just going to brush my hair and then get dressed," Cyg managed to murmur.

"The maid came in with riding clothes for you. Shall I bring them to you?" His eyes glinted over her.

"Uh . . . I was going to wear my dungarees." She watched him carefully.

"Sounds good." He reached down and took the brush from her hands. Silence stretched between them as he bent to the task of unsnarling her hair, letting the burnished curls fall through his fingers.

"Will you wear sneakers and not boots?" he muttered, lowering his head over her fragrant hair, his eyes closing.

"Huh?" Cyg leaned back against him. "Ah . . . yes. That's all I ever used when I rode."

He smiled down at her, his hand still in her hair. "Indulge me on that and let me get you some boots. It's safer."

"All right." She gulped, watching his face come closer as he bent to kiss her, his tongue touching hers.

He wasn't gone too long and the rhythm of her heart was almost back to normal when he returned. Cyg was dressed in faded dungarees that hugged her bottom like a second skin. The long-sleeved blouse was plaid and with it she wore a suede jerkin that would keep her warm in the brisk May morning.

She stared open-mouthed at the boots Darius was carrying, a matching pair to those on his own feet. "You are not going to tell me that you just whipped up a matching pair of boots."

Darius grinned. "Phil keeps many things in stock for his guests; boots are one of them."

"Ah, yes, the idle rich," Cyg muttered, pulling the supple leather over her feet.

"Phil is not the most ambitious person I've ever met, but some of the rich do work very hard." He stared at her, unsmiling.

Cyg gazed up at him. "I . . . I didn't mean to insult you." She started to rise.

Darius caught her close to him. "I know you didn't. For some reason I'm just more sensitive about everything you say." He bent over her. "You have a strange effect on me, lady. I don't know if I like it." His mouth closed over hers, the kiss deepening, his tongue coaxing her lips apart.

"Cygnet," he groaned, his hand coming up to explore her breast.

"Riding," she squeaked.

Darius removed his lips slowly from hers. "This time we'll do it your way . . . next time we do it mine," he snarled softly into her neck, taking tiny bites of the taut skin.

She tried to smile, but her face felt rubbery, as though nothing on her body would listen to any command she gave it.

They left the room, hand in hand, their bodies close to one another, their hips bumping as they descended the stairs.

Outside, Cyg took a deep breath of the fresh spring air, glad of her vest in the sudden bite of the wind.

"Cold, darling?" Darius bent over her as they approached the stables.

She shook her head, wanting to look into his emerald eyes forever.

"Mr. Chadwick?" A bandy legged man with a bald head called to Darius. When Darius lifted his head, the man spat tobacco from the side of his mouth into some bushes. "I'm Ceveck. I have the horses you wanted." The man ran his eyes over Cyg as he led a dapple gray mare up to her. "Here, let me give you a leg up miss."

"No," Darius barked, his face cold. "Just get my horse, I'll take care of this."

Cyg was about to throw herself over the saddle as she used to do as a child, when Darius was there, mumbling, "putting his hands on you." She turned to look at him as he lifted her into the saddle. "What did you say?"

"Nothing." He glared up at her. "I shouldn't have let you wear those jeans. They're too tight . . . they're like a second skin," he growled. He pushed his hand through his hair and frowned as if puzzled.

Cyg laughed, making him glower at her before a

smile creased his face. "That's better. Now you don't look like a bear."

"You're too beautiful." He swung into the saddle, shifting sideways on the big chested bay stallion to look at her. "You have me off balance, lady. I don't like the feeling."

She shouted with laughter, digging her heels into the mare, happy when the animal jumped forward into a run. Cyg knew that she had never been so happy. Yet there was fear mixed with that joy; she quickly buried the black thought that could mar the day.

They rode for miles and though Cyg had the impression that the landscape was most attractive, she really didn't see anything except Darius.

They stopped once and tethered the horses.

When Darius took her into his arms, she went gladly, her mouth open and seeking on his. When she heard his groan of satisfaction, she felt her heart kick into overdrive. They sank down onto the ground.

"We can't stay here." Darius shifted her until she was lying on top of him. "Too damp." His mouth nibbled at her neck.

"Right." Cyg moaned kissing his face with short rubbing caresses.

They rose, still holding one another.

"I've known you fifteen years . . . twenty maybe." Cyg burbled, her fingers tracing his jaw line, watching a muscle jump in his cheek.

"One hundred last Wednesday," Darius muttered. "This is crazy. I stopped necking years ago."

"Fun, huh?" Cyg gripped his hair between her hands with a gentle fierceness.

"You make me feel as if I'm full of helium." Darius groaned. "Weird." He brushed some leaves from her dungarees, then lifted her into the saddle. "With you now I feel like I'm reliving every Christmas and every birthday of my life." His upturned face was flushed as he stood next to her saddle, his hands still at her waist. "Stupid, isn't it?"

"No." Cyg leaned down and touched his chin. "Lovely."

Darius mounted his horse, spending a few moments to steady the nervous stallion.

They rode and talked, they stopped and walked. They drank the fruit juice Darius had brought in his saddlebags. They talked about books. Darius shared her liking of Joseph Heller and Joseph Wambaugh, Shakespeare and Yeats. She argued about music.

"How can you prefer the moderns over Beethoven?"

"Gershwin was the greatest," Darius said.

"Ohhh, don't be so smug." Cyg tried to glare at him but found herself smiling at him instead. She had never been with anyone who had made her feel so confident, so serene, yet so excited.

A voice deep within her said that he would be gone tomorrow just as she would be, that his world did not fit with hers. She tried to stifle that voice. She wanted nothing to intrude. She wouldn't listen to anything that would spoil her time with Darius.

When they returned to the house, the buffet lunch had already been cleared away. Somehow Darius managed to find them some rolls and sliced ham and they ate the food picnic-style with more fruit juice.

"Wouldn't you rather have beer . . . or something?" Cyg asked.

Darius had found a lap robe in his car and spread it on the patio near the unopened outdoor pool. No one was around. They were alone there. He rolled over on his stomach, not spilling a drop from his glass. "I remember the drastic effect alcohol has on you, angel . . ." He ducked as Cyg aimed a fist at him. ". . . so I decided we would stick with soft drinks today."

"Martyr."

Darius nodded. "I am truly noble." His face was solemn but his eyes were alight with mirth.

"You look very smug." Cyg tried not to laugh at him.

"You're confused," Darius insisted, reaching toward her mouth. "You have mustard . . . there." He kissed the spot. "I've had a wonderful day." He glanced at his watch, then gave her a rueful look. "And it's almost over."

"It can't be. We just had lunch."

"We were late." Darius wound his arm around her waist and pulled her close. "It's five o'clock. We should change for cocktails soon." He pulled back from her. "Generally I hate this type of gathering, but now I find that instead of being bored, I want to do everything I can to stop the clock." His brows rose quizzically.

Cyg looked away from him. "Have you been to many weekend parties like this?"

"Some." Darius turned her head with one finger. "I have never found a woman like you at any of these parties, though, under any conditions."

Cyg allowed him to pull her back against him even though she felt an uncomfortable wriggle of doubt deep inside her.

They spoke of everything. Cyg even told him about the ratty tailed cat she had had as a child and how heartbroken she was when the doctors discovered she had an allergy to cat hair. "My parents didn't have the heart to put him to sleep so they gave him to my aunt. She kept him until he died at the ripe old age of fifteen. Rufus was a good cat."

"I had a dog like that when I was a boy. My father had him put down when I went off to college. He was old." Darius's voice was casual, but his mouth tightened and his eyes took on a faraway look.

"You loved him." Cyg leaned over him, kissing

his face where a swath of chestnut hair fell forward onto his forehead.

He looked up at her, kissing her hand. "Yes . . . I loved that mutt." He gazed at her unsmiling. "And I never told anyone that story." He stared at her. "I think *I'm* the confused one."

Cyg cradled his head against her breast, feeling a fierce love for the young man who came home to find his dog had been put to sleep.

They sat in silence, holding each other, looking at the pink tinged May sky, not feeling the bite of the breeze.

When they finally rose to leave, it was as if there was an unspoken agreement between them.

They approached other groups of people staying at Phil's, but although they didn't ignore them, neither did they make an effort to join them.

They parted in front of Cyg's room, Darius kissing her over and over again.

She was already in the shower when she heard Kim enter the bedroom.

She was drying her hair when Kim asked, "So, where have you been all day? Phil wanted to introduce you to some of his friends." She frowned. "Honestly, Cyg, I wish you wouldn't disappear. Phil gets mad at me then."

Cyg shrugged. "I was with Darius."

"Wow, are you lucky. He has more money than Croesus." Kim sighed, forgetting her irritation. "I wish he would take an interest in me."

Cyg felt a shaft of pain at the thought of Darius being with Kim or anyone else. She looked down, letting her hair fall forward so that Kim wouldn't read the expression she knew would be on her face.

"What dress are you wearing tonight, Cyg? I noticed that Phil left two each for us." She looked smug. "I'll bet the other girls don't have two." She tapped Cyg on the shoulder. "You're lucky you're with me."

Cyg smiled but said nothing, shivering as that

uncomfortable feeling she had had before, overtook her again. She wished she had met Darius under other circumstances.

She left the bathroom and walked to the closet where two dresses were hanging side by side, shoes and accessories on a shelf.

She wore the least revealing of the two, an apricot-colored cheongsam, slit to the thigh on both sides with long sleeves. The Oriental silk clung to her body delineating each curve and depression. *Peau de soie* shoes were in a deeper shade of apricot and a small clutch purse the same color and fabric as the dress completed the outfit. She piled her blond hair on top of her head, coronet style, allowing two curls to fall near her ears. She wore no jewelry, except a pinkie ring of wrought gold that had belonged to her grandmother.

"Cyg!" Kim cried. "You look too plain . . . like an empress or or something . . ."

Cyg whirled to face her, making an effort to smile. "That's a contradiction in terms, I think."

"You know what I mean." Kim grimaced. "Phil likes us to dress a certain way. You know, more skin."

Cyg ground her teeth. "This dress is fine. After all Phil included this in his selection, didn't he?"

"Yes, I guess so." Kim frowned at her. "I wish you wouldn't talk in that . . . that college way you have. I went to school, too, you know."

"Sorry." Cyg pressed her lips together. There was no point in telling Kim that she felt increasingly uncomfortable about being at Phil's place. She knew that if it weren't for Darius being here, she would leave. She didn't listen to the voice that said Run . . . *run* from him. He's the real jeopardy.

"Okay." Kim shrugged and went back into the bathroom.

Cyg looked at the small gold watch her parents had given her on her graduation from college and took a deep breath. It was time to go downstairs. Darius would be waiting for her. That thought made her move more rapidly out of the room, along the hall, and down the stairs.

She paused halfway down the staircase. Darius was standing in the foyer leaning against the wall, a vibrant redhead at his side. Cyg had to take deep breaths to dissipate the swelling pain in her chest. She stood there looking down at the two of them.

Even to her jaded gaze, it didn't look as though Darius was flirting with the girl. He was nodding his head, the corners of his mouth lifted in a soft steely smile as the redhead gestured, laughed, and postured in what Cyg thought was a disgustingly provocative way. She had the strongest urge to rush down the stairs, grab the vase of some twenty roses from the Louis Quinze table in the hall, and upend the vase on that red head.

Inhaling deeply, she glided down the rest of the flight of stairs, head high, biting her inner lip to keep from screaming at the redheaded hussy to unhand her Darius.

Darius looked up, straightened from the wall, his face smiling, his eyes watchful.

Cyg stopped at the bottom step, letting her eyes widen to their fullest. "Have I kept you waiting, darling?"

"Yes," Darius drawled, appreciative amusement a green glitter in his eyes. He inclined his head toward the redhead who was now staring at Cyg angrily. He murmured something and strolled toward Cyg. "But it was worth the wait," he muttered, bending to brush his mouth across hers. "Hellcat."

"Nothing of the kind," Cyg mumbled back, raising her chin so that Darius would have freer access to her neck. "I haven't scratched her eyes out."

"No, you haven't done that." He put his arm around her, not looking back at the redhead who was still standing there glaring at Cyg. "Let me get you a drink, darling. Tonight it will be soda I think."

"I prefer Saratoga water and lime, if you can find it," she cooed at him, knowing she sounded silly, but not able to help herself.

"When you talk to me like that and look like that, you could ask me for a gold Rolls Royce. I'd get it for you today."

Cyg felt chilled in the green heat of those eyes. "I don't want anything like that," she whispered through stiff lips. "Just the Saratoga water, please." Bile rose in her throat.

"What is it, angel? You look so pale all of a sudden." He slipped his arm around her, bending over her.

"Nothing." Cyg tried to smile. "Just thirsty."

Darius didn't leave right away. He watched her for a few moments longer, then he kissed her cheek. "One Saratoga water and lime, coming up."

For the first time since they had met yesterday, Cyg wasn't on tenterhooks until he returned to her. She needed time to pull herself together, to think. Call girl, call girl . . . she shook her head to clear it. Damn the fate that let her meet Darius this way.

She wandered out onto the terrace, the cool breeze off the Sound making her shiver. She was glad she had worn the long-sleeved dress and rubbed her arms. She looked at the ball of sun in the western sky. You should be long gone from here, Cyg my girl, she told herself. Why are you staying? Because Darius is here . . . Oh, don't tell me I'm not smart, she retorted to the little voice inside. I know it isn't smart, but . . . she took a deep breath, feeling the light of the sun enter her body. Darius . . . Darius . . . He is worth the risk she was taking in getting hurt. Getting hurt is putting it mildly, she thought. When she lost him, she would ache forever.

"Cyg." Phil took hold of her arm. "Don't tell me Darius isn't at your side."

"He went to get us drinks."

"Have my staff been lax? I'll have to speak to them." Phil spoke in an absentminded way, his eyes roving her body. "You are one beautiful lady, Cyg."

"Thank you." She turned away, not liking the way he was looking at her.

"Don't turn away from me like that," Phil snarled. "You were paid to come out here . . . and paid pretty well, too."

Cyg whirled back to face him. "Yes, you paid me to keep your guests company, and I'm doing that . . . but don't get any ideas about me, Phil. Nobody buys me! Nobody!" She could feel her nostrils flare as she inhaled an angry breath.

"You're even more beautiful when you're angry."

"Banal."

"What?" Phil's mouth twisted in irritation.

"Banal. Your conversation and you . . . banal!" Cyg said sweetly.

"Why you—" Phil's hands rose.

"Something wrong, darling?" Darius's voice was velvet-sheathed steel. He set two glasses down on a nearby table and approached her, his hands hanging loose at his sides, walking slightly forward, his eyes on Phil. "You look upset, angel," he grated out, still looking at Phil. "Haven't I made it plain enough that Cygnet is with me?"

She bit her bottom lip while watching him. She could almost smell and taste the menace emanating from his body. She sniffed as though she would be able to detect the sulfur in the air, as though Darius had suddenly become a visitor from the netherworld. "No . . . no Darius, it's all right." She looked at Phil, who stared at Darius bitterly.

"Take it easy, Darius." Phil put up a hand. "This isn't Yale and, unlike my brother, I was not on the boxing team." His lips had a flaccid look to them when he smiled. "I'm a lover not a fighter."

"The next time you come near Cyg," Darius snarled each syllable of the words, "be prepared to be a fighter. I don't like the way she looks when you're around. Get lost."

"This is my house," Phil blustered.

"Then we'll leave," Darius barked.

"Now wait, Darius," Phil wheedled, "you promised you'd look at the specs for—"

"If you want me to stay, then you give Cygnet a wide berth." Darius jabbed a finger at the other man, his body almost in front of Cyg's. "I mean it."

Phil held up both hands, palms forward. "Sure, sure . . . that's all right by me. No harm done." Phil left, neither looking at Cyg nor speaking to her.

"Okay, darling?" Darius turned around and put his arms about her, his lips running down her cheek.

Sighing, Cyg lifted her arms and wound them around his neck. "I'm fine now."

"I didn't know where you went." He nuzzled her neck above the mandarin collar. "I hated it." There was surprise in his voice.

She leaned back from him and watched the emotion in his face. "I didn't like it when you were gone, either." She snuggled against him, delighting in the feel of that hard body against her.

Darius led her back to the table to get her drink. He sipped it first, then handed it to her. "Saratoga water with lime. They had to get it out of the cellar." He raised his brows. "It doesn't taste half bad . . . and I'll probably like the effect it has on you better than the wine."

"I don't fall asleep when I drink Saratoga water." Cyg chuckled.

"Thank heaven." His eyes were a liquid heat.

They stayed by themselves until dinner was announced. When Darius discovered that he and Cyg were not seated at the same table, he promptly had their seat cards changed. Cyg laughed at his high-handedness.

"Is this the way you handle all the obstacles in your life, like a hurricane?"

"Yes." He grinned as he helped her into her chair. There were eight other persons at the round table and though Darius spoke to the others and introduced Cyg, he made it plain that he was only interested in talking to her. Since the others all had companions as well, this was no problem.

Cyg didn't count the number of round tables in the room, but she guessed that there were more than two hundred people sitting down to dinner. Her discomfort increased as she gazed around the room and saw many assessing eyes on her. If only she could take Darius by the hand and disappear from there, she thought ruefully.

"Don't you like the lobster, angel?" Darius whispered to her, his face close to hers.

"Yes . . . I like it." Cyg bent to her food, knowing she would never be able to tell Darius how she felt. After all, she had come here of her own free will. He thought she was like the others. She shivered at the hated thought.

Dinner was an ordeal to her. She felt as if thousands of eyes were fixed on her and though reason told her this wasn't so, she couldn't rid herself of the sensation. By the time the rich *bombe* was served for dessert, Cyg's stomach was churning. Not all Darius's coaxing could get her to eat the sweet.

It was a relief to leave the table. She and Darius wandered hand in hand into the solarium to dance.

When he took her in his arms, she pushed her worries away and concentrated on the feel of that hard body against hers. She let her fingers wander over his neck, twisting up into the straight thick hair at his nape.

"You have lights in your hair," she murmured to him, eyes half closed. "I like your hair."

"Do you, darling?" His lips nuzzled her ear.

"Yes. You have sexy hair," she burbled, loving the feel of his mouth against her skin.

"You have sexy everything," he muttered.

"Good."

"Good?" Darius laughed, lifting his head, the hot glint in his eyes belying the amusement in his voice. "You keep surprising me."

"Yes," Cyg said. "For the first time in my life, I find myself wanting to be sexy. Awful, huh?"

"Wonderful. Just make sure you only feel that way with me."

Cyg pretended to consider his words. When she felt his one hand swat her behind, she giggled. Strange, she had never remembered giggling before she met Darius.

They danced everything: the polka, the tango, the waltz. Cyg was breathless with laughter when he whirled her around him in a fast jitterbug. "Where did you learn that?"

"My aunts." Darius laughed down at her, his arms cushioning her from the other dancers. "They were wild ones in their day and they are firmly convinced that anyone who was not brought up during the big band era was raised a deprived child."

Cyg leaned on him.

"Tired, darling?" Darius's voice was soft.

"A little." She looked up at him, feeling her heart race out of control.

"I'll take you up to my room."

"Yes." Cyg pushed away the warning voices inside her. Nothing was going to interfere between her and Darius. She would never see him again. She sensed that, but she wanted him to love her anyway. She loved him. She was sure. She wanted to be loved by him and give him her love in return. Oh, yes she was sure!

They danced out onto the terrace. The breeze had died but the night was still cool. Darius's arm around her kept her warm.

Cyg stopped. "Would you mind if we stopped in my room first? I want to get something." She remembered the lovely silky nightgown that Kim had pointed out as Cyg's.

Darius nodded and walked with her to the room, coming inside and watching when she went to the closet to remove the filmy gown from the drawer there.

"For me?" Darius whispered.

"For you," Cyg answered.

A few moments later in Darius's room, Cyg looked this way and that at her mirror image, aware that she had never worn such exquisite nor such revealing nightwear. Her usual was flannel pajamas in winter, cotton shorties in summer. The pure silk in a flesh color seemed like her own skin. The gown clung to her body as though the outer layer was a magnet pulling the light-as-air fabric to her form. Her breasts were barely hidden by the almost diaphanous material, her legs seductively outlined.

"Why don't you feel embarrassed?" she muttered to her mirror image. "Why aren't you a nervous wreck about going to bed with a man you've only just met?" She shrugged at the mirror, her smile widening at the dreamy look on her face. "You look like a fool," she scolded herself in a whisper, but her twin in the glass lifted one shoulder again. "I love him. I don't know how, and I sure as blazes don't know why, but I love him." She sighed. "I wish I could remember my Yeats. Oh, Darius I don't know why I love you but I do . . ." She was going to give the mirror a more defined argument, but the door to the bathroom opened and Darius walked through, still rubbing his head with a towel. My, he was quick, she thought bemusedly, as she whirled from the mirror to face him, feeling strong and sure, delighting in the way his eyes focused on her at once.

He flung the towel behind him in a careless gesture, a muscle jumping in his lower jaw. "You're too beautiful to be real, angel." His rough whisper crossed the room like a jet of fire, igniting her skin. "I'm afraid if I tell you to come here, you'll disappear in a puff of pink smoke." The thread of amusement in his voice had a tremor to it.

"I won't disappear." Cyg lifted her arms and floated to him, loving the leaping heat of those green eyes as he opened his arms to receive her.

"Cygnet, darling, you're everything a man could want," he muttered into her neck, before he swung her up into his arms. He held her for long moments, just staring at her. "If you're a figment of my imagination, for Heaven's sake then don't tell me."

As he carried her to the bed in slow measured steps, not taking his eyes from her, Cyg felt her first shiver of fear. Oh, it wasn't Darius she feared. It was the memory of Len Peters and his rough, laughing handling of her virginity. His treatment had made her vow she would never give herself to any man unless she had the upper hand.

Now, here she was, giving herself to Darius with no thought of anything but how to please him.

"What is it, love? I felt you tremble." Darius laid her gently on the bed, stripping the toweling wrap from his own body as he followed her down. "Don't be afraid of me. I'll be gentle with you. I'd never want to hurt you."

Cyg lifted her hand to his chestnut hair, loving the thickness of it under her fingers. "I know that. It wasn't you that made me shudder. It was remembering another person, another time."

Anger filled Darius's face as he lay above her, the hand stroking her deep blond hair, clenching in the curls. "Whoever the hell he is, don't think of him! God, I could kill him, whoever he is!" Darius put his face next to hers, muttering love words into her ear. "I've never felt like this," he growled.

Sighing with warm delight, Cyg folded her arms around him, holding him close to her. "He is forgotten. He was a momentary unpleasantness . . . gone . . . never to have been." Her words slurred as heat filled her body.

Darius let his mouth rove over her, not attempting to remove the silky flesh-colored gown.

Cyg's body trembled as Darius kissed each of her toes, his mouth lingering over them as though he would minister to them. His mouth forced the silken length of gown up her body, making Cyg gasp as power began to fill her own body. "Darius!" she heard someone moan, then realized it was her own voice. She felt the brush of cooling air over the lower portion of her body, the intimate kiss making her arch in surprise. The pleasure was there: It was growing, building in her like an explosion of delight. Tremors pulsated the length and breadth of her as inch by inch he loved her body, as centimeter by centimeter he turned her to liquid flame.

She reached for his head with a trembling strength, wanting his mouth against hers, body to body, eyes to eyes.

All at once his hands cupped her shape under his, the moisture of their bodies mingling, adding an eroticism to their movements that made Cyg feel as though she had melted into Darius.

The sensual expertise of Darius's lovemaking changed. Shudders wracked his body as his mouth gentled on hers. "Never . . . never . . . my Cygnet has it been like this. Never," Darius muttered, his face pressed between her breasts. His body coaxed and nurtured hers as they approached the tunnel of love where they would be alone. He entered her body as though she were a temple and he would worship her.

His restraint made Cyg turn into a volcano of flaming need. She grasped at him, her hips lifted, telling him with a writhing message that she didn't want him to hold back any more . . . that she wanted the hard, masculine thrust of his body.

She felt the implosion of his body within her, crying out loud in her own blissful satisfaction.

"You're beautiful, Cygnet. I love everything about you." Darius's voice had a husky quality, his breathing still harsh.

"You're beautiful, too," Cyg crooned, her eyes fluttering closed, her head pillowed on his chest. The last thing she heard was the rumble of his chuckle under her ear as he whispered to her, "But baby, we've just started."

Through the night, Darius woke her and each time she met him with a want as deep as his own. "I never knew . . . I never knew . . ." he slurred the words against her all through the night.

In the morning she woke, sun streaming across her face, a pot of steaming coffee on a tray on the bedside table, a jug of iced orange juice as well. She could feel herself smile as she read the note: SLEEPYHEAD, DIDN'T WANT TO WAKEN YOU. YOU SLEEP LIKE A BABY. BE BACK TO BREAKFAST WITH YOU BEFORE YOU MISS ME. LOVE, DARIUS.

She drank all the juice and some of the coffee, then skipped to the bathroom, humming and doing ballet pirouettes as she ran the shower. She had never felt so happy. She laughed out loud as she recalled how she had hated coming to Phil Tabor's party. Now all she wanted to do was stand under the shower and daydream of Darius.

Three

Cyg gave a yelp of surprise when she realized the water in the shower had turned cold. "How long have I been in here daydreaming about Darius?" She shivered, reaching for one of the warmed bath sheets. "Lord, Cyg Melton, you are getting worse and worse." She glared at herself after she wiped a clear patch in the steamy mirror. "Get dressed, fool."

She was sure that Darius would have already breakfasted without her, but she hurried into her old jeans and a fresh blouse anyway. They could have coffee together, she thought as she skipped out of the room, sun high and cloud light.

Once downstairs, she went right to the large dining area where there would be a breakfast buffet. Darius wasn't there. Perhaps he had eaten with someone else and was out golfing or horseback riding. She sighed. Taking a blueberry muffin and a cup of coffee from the sideboard she went out onto terrace that edged that portion of the house.

There was a slight breeze, but the sun was so warming that Cyg was glad she hadn't worn a jacket.

She wandered down onto the grounds toward a garden area.

"Well, well, don't tell me you're alone for a change." Phil Tabor's voice had a truculence to it that made Cyg eye him warily.

"I was looking for Darius." She sipped at her coffee after finishing the muffin.

"Really? He's around somewhere."

"I'll look for him." Cyg tried to move past Phil, but took hold of her arm.

"I didn't like the way you talked to me last night." His hand gripped her tightly.

Cyg tried to pry his hand from her arm. "Let me go." She glared up at him. "For the record, I didn't like the way you talked to me either."

"You were paid to come here," Phil snarled.

"Nobody buys me. Now let me go. We've been through this before."

"You have pretty uppity ways for a street lady," Phil snapped.

Cyg gasped. Before she could even think about it, anger filled her and she brought her other arm up, her hand in a closed fist. She struck Phil on the side of the face, hurting her hand, and making him reel back and release his hold on her.

"You bitch . . . you lousy bitch." He growled, trying to grab her again.

Cyg took off at a run, angry hurt coursing through her. "How dare he say that to me . . . how dare he!" She could feel tears of fury on her face as she ran. She wouldn't stay here!

When she reached the other side of the house, she stopped and put a shaking hand to her mouth as she tried to catch her breath. "Damn him."

She saw two men coming toward her and turned and walked at an angle away from them, not changing direction when one of them called to her.

The only person she wanted to be with was Darius. She *needed* to be with him.

Wandering idly through the lovely grounds, she gave desultory glances to the profusion of flowers. When she saw a shadowy copse of trees, she wondered whether she was dressed warm enough to enter its cool depths. Looking around her again to see if she might catch sight of Darius, she sighed when she didn't and decided that she would just enter the outer fringes of the woods, since it would, no doubt, be damp and cold.

There was an eerie misty smell as she entered the darkened mini forest, but it was not unpleasant. There were violet-like flowers on the moldy leaf floor of the wood and Cyg bent to gather a few, knowing full well that they would die quickly, as all wild flowers did.

She was humming to herself and picking, bent over to her task when she heard the muffled thud of horses hooves coming her way. She was about to straighten to see who it was when one of the unknown horsemen spoke from the perimeter of the woods.

"Phuuu, I needed that gallop. My head was still fuzzy from last night," the first unknown man said.

"Didn't the lady love Phil provided for you clear your head a little?" the second horseman asked.

Cyg froze in her bent-over position.

"Are you kidding? She was pretty coked up by the time we got to bed. Oh, don't get me wrong, I'm not complaining about my little bird. She was good. I may use her again tonight."

"That's the difference between us, Chuck. I like a little variety on these weekends, even if it is a little expensive."

"I like the variety . . . and the privacy. Phil provides both." There was creak of saddle leather as though the speaker shifted on his saddle. "I wouldn't want my wife in on this. What do you think that little dolly that hangs around Phil so much would cost me?"

"There's Phil. Hey, Phil . . . Ask him yourself. Maybe he's through with her." The laughter was crowlike, making Cyg shiver. "Phil, Ron, here, wants to know what his chances are with Kim for this evening."

Cyg heard the rustle of paper and chanced a look, seeing money change hands though she couldn't see faces.

"I think your chances are pretty good . . . now." Phil's laugh sent a shudder down Cyg's spine.

"Bud was eyeing Dar Chadwick's lady, Phil. I'll bet his chances aren't so good in that quarter."

"Ah, yes. Cyg Melton. Darius always had good taste in women, but I don't think I'll take your money for that, Bud." Phil's voice was gruff. "You haven't the money to outbid Darius. He's interested enough to pay top dollar. I know him."

"Hell, we all have nice taste in women, Tabor. In fact, I'm willing to up it a thousand for the blond." His laugh was like a raucous whip to Cyg's nerves. "I'm going to ask the lady if she wouldn't like a nice change of pace tonight."

Laughter faded as the horses and riders moved away.

Cyg sank to her knees on the wet ground, her hands crossed over her stomach. She was a whore! To those men she was a woman for hire! A prostitute! She retched and was sick on the mucky ground.

She had no idea how long she knelt there, seeing pictures of herself that made her writhe in shame. That man said he was going to *use* the unknown girl again tonight. *Use* was the operative word, Cyg thought, bile rising in her throat again. Darius would pay top dollar!

She gagged again as she remembered that the man called Bud was going to approach her that very evening.

"I have to get away from here." She pushed the words from her sour mouth.

Wiping her lips with a tissue she yanked from her blouse pocket, she stood up, a shaking hand pressed to her face. She tried to think, but her brain was sawdust.

She knew that if the man came up to her that evening when Darius was present there would be an argument if not a fight. Darius would not stand the insult. Cyg was sure of that. Already she sensed his proprietary attitude toward her, his possessive way of keeping her away from the others. Yet in reality wasn't that how he thought of her? A party girl? A call girl he'd bought and paid for?

"After today, I'll just hold Darius in my mind, deep and beautiful . . ." Like a flash, the poem she had been trying to remember flooded her mind. She mumbled the words to herself. ". . . for everything that's lovely is but a brief, dreamy kind of delight." She finished the Yeats poem on a sob.

As she turned to leave the copse of trees, the flowers she had picked spilled from her hand. She stared at the crumpled blossoms as if she was bidding them a sad farewell.

She stumbled back into the sunlight, one hand shading her eyes.

She had no idea how she got to the tennis courts, but when she saw Kim playing there with a man she recalled seeing at the party the night before, Cyg didn't respond to Kim's wave. Instead she pretended not to see her roommate and walked quickly away, skirting the swimming pool and striding toward the house.

"Cygnet . . . Cygnet."

Cyg turned around and saw Darius loping toward her, a relieved look on his face.

He came right up to her and took her in his arms. "I couldn't find you," he mumbled into her hair. "It was bad."

Cyg clung to him, her fingers biting into his shoulders, her face pressed tight to his chest.

"Darling, what is it? Are you cold? You're shivering." Darius leaned back from her, concern on his face deepening to a frown as he watched her. "What happened? You're pale." He looked up, his eyes narrowing as he gazed around him. "Was somebody bothering you?"

"No . . . no." She struggled to keep her voice even. "I didn't know where you were. I guess I waited too long before having something to eat."

"I'm sorry, angel. I was talking to Phil. I told him I was in a hurry to have lunch with you. He told me if he saw you he would tell you I was on the patio."

"I see," Cyg said, recalling vividly that Phil had not given Darius's message to her. "Why were you talking to Phil?" She tried to clear the hoarseness from her throat.

Darius waved his hand, a look of irritation on his craggy face. "I owed him some money for . . . never mind. And he wanted to talk about some damn fool deal he's trying to make me sink money into. Let's not talk about him."

"No, let's not." She leaned against him as he slipped an arm around her waist. "Do you think we might sneak something from the kitchen and eat by ourselves?"

"Sounds great." Darius kissed the top of her head. "On second thought, why don't we drive to a little place I know on the tip of the island. How does that sound?"

"Wonderful." She grabbed at his shoulders again with both hands. "Darius, I'm a little muddy, but I don't even want to change. Let's drive to that place right now."

Darius's face lit with a smile so boyish that Cyg caught her breath. "All right, lady, your chariot awaits. Let's go." He swung her high in his arms, carrying her across the lawn with long sure strides.

Cyg looped her arms around his neck, closing her eyes, burying her thoughts. She would have him for such a little while. She wasn't going to think of the future . . . the empty blackness that would be hers when Darius was no longer with her. She could never let him be part of her life now. He thought of her as a call girl, just as those men on the horses near the woods thought of the other girls here. No, whore was the word. The thought of that faceless man approaching her this evening and asking her to change from Darius to himself made her tighten her arms convulsively around Darius's neck.

"Hey, lady, I don't mind if you choke me, but why not wait until we're alone." Darius chuckled, carrying her past staring men and women, looking neither left nor right, even when some called to him.

"Sorry." Cyg loosened her grip on his neck, glad that he didn't put her down until they were at the back entrance to the house.

"I'm not," he murmured into her ear, still keeping his arm around her as they entered the kitchen area. "I love your arms around me." He lifted his head and smiled at the uniformed woman cutting vegetables into a colander. "Maggie, cancel the brunch for two, I'm taking Miss Melton on an outing."

"All right, Mr. Chadwick." The woman smiled at Cyg before going back to her vegetables.

Even the woman's friendliness made Cyg's skin crawl. What was Maggie really thinking? What was her opinion of the women who came to Phil Tabor's parties? Cyg shuddered.

"Darling, are you coming down with something?" Darius pulled her closer to his body. "Maybe we should get you a sweater."

"No . . . no." Cyg fought the panic she could hear in her own voice. She tried to smile when he looked at her sharply. "I . . . I just want us to be alone. If we stay here for even a minute, someone will come and want to talk to you, maybe. Let's go now."

"Now it is." Darius grinned at her, but there

was still a crease of concern in his forehead when he looked at her.

Cyg wanted to run to his car even though she didn't know which was his.

She didn't relax until Darius unlocked a silver Ferrari and helped her into the passenger seat. She was too immersed in her own misery to pay more than passing interest to the lush interior of the high-powered car. She watched Darius's hands instead as he turned on the ignition and drove the car out of its space and down the drive toward the highway.

He looked over at her as they approached the open gates to the highway that ran along the front of the property. Darius let the car idle as he waited for a tractor trailer truck to lumber by. "When I think how close I came to not coming here this weekend it makes me sweat in fright. God, darling, it would have been horrible if I hadn't been here." His teeth came together with a snap.

Cyg studied the intent look on his face. "It would have been the worst thing in the world for me if you hadn't been here this weekend, Darius." She spoke in measured tones, her voice vibrating back to her in the enclosed area.

"Lord, you're lovely." He leaned over to kiss her nose, before checking the traffic once more and pulling out onto the highway.

Another truck was just rounding the curve and the honking bellow as he warned Darius of his approach, sounded angry.

"I try to give these fellows a wide berth," Darius said, throwing her a smile as he geared down and let the car gain speed. "They're too big for me."

Cyg smiled at him, edging as close to him as the gearshift would allow.

Darius reached over to put his hand on her thigh. "I have always loved this car until now. Right at this moment, I would gladly exchange it for any car with a wide seat where my lady could cuddle up to me."

"Your lady would like that as well."

Darius threw her a quick glance, then looked back at the traffic, a muscle jumping at the corner of his jaw. "Cygnet, please don't look at me like that."

"Like what?" She smothered her dark feelings inside of her and let only Darius surface in her mind.

"Like a beautiful Circe." His voice had a throaty quality that set Cyg's pulses galloping.

They drove for long curving miles, not fast not slow, Darius lifting her hand every so often to press kisses into the palm.

The restaurant that Darius chose was a renovated farmhouse that had a Landmark sign out in front and a mounting block near the drive. There were few cars in the crushed stone parking lot and when they entered the barroom, Cyg gasped with delight at the smoke-blackened beams in the ceiling and the large open fireplace that had whole logs burning in it. The bar was aged oak. One customer sat there talking with the bartender, who nodded to them as they passed through into the dining room.

Darius chuckled when Cyg whispered, "It looks like George Washington slept here."

They were ushered to a table near the window, white dotted swiss curtains letting the afternoon sun filter into the room, making the table seem their own corner of the world.

Darius hitched his chair closer to hers and lifted one of her hands between the two of his. "Your fingers are so slender, so lovely. Do you model your hands?" He kissed each finger, not stopping what he was doing even when an older woman wearing a crisp white apron and a white mob cap on her head, stood next to their table holding two long narrow menus in her hand.

She coughed.

Darius looked up and grinned. "We'll have a Dom . . ."

"We have a fine Riesling '77, sir," the woman said, her voice firm.

"Fine." Darius lifted his arm to stop her from leaving. "And bring us two of your specials, please."

"Today, sir, it is . . ."

"Whatever it is will be fine." Darius smiled at the woman and received an appreciative smile in return. Then he looked back at Cyg. "I might buy a sign that reads . . ." He put his hand, palm out, in an arc in front of him: "DARIUS WANTS TO BE ALONE WITH CYG." He leaned over and kissed her cheek. "Is that all right with you?"

"Fine." Cyg felt breathless. She loved the feeling of power it gave her to reach up and run her finger down his jaw. The fresh shaved smoothness under her skin had a dizzying effect on her and made Darius's face flush with desire.

"Tonight we'll dance and hold each other . . ." Darius began.

"Let's not talk about tonight," Cyg snapped, then bit her lip when she saw the sharp-eyed puzzlement on his face. "What I meant was . . ." Cyg swallowed, then plowed ahead, "I don't want to talk about time passing. Just let's think about each minute that we're together now." She pulled Darius's hand up to her cheek and held it there. "Please."

"Yes." He stared at her, his eyes going over each feature. "It was your face that knocked me out the first time I saw you. I couldn't believe that anyone could look like a willowy blond angel. Your curls were swinging about your face like a golden cloud. Your smile was unsure, but so sweet." He chuckled. "I stampeded across the room like a bull at the charge. I must have rolled over three people at least but I didn't stop until I reached you. I was afraid someone else would get to you first."

Cyg felt a wrench at his words, at the mention of other men trying to get to her. It seemed to her that Darius, in his own mind, thought of her as a call girl, even though he had never intimated such a thing out loud. She smiled at him with great effort, remembering her promise to herself that she would enjoy every moment she had with him. She let her hand rove his face. She would have to leave but until she did, she was going to treasure every moment with Darius.

When the food came, it was duckling, the tenderest, flakiest meat of that fowl she had ever tasted. The dressing was apple, orange, and a spiced bread mixture that had a succulent aroma and taste. The Riesling was dry, light and fruity.

Neither of them wanted dessert, and they drank their coffee hurriedly.

When they left the restaurant, Darius holding her close to his side, Cyg turned for a last look at the building.

"Darling, don't be sad. We'll be coming back again . . . as many times as you like," Darius said softly as he opened the car door for her.

Instead of slipping into her seat, she turned in his arms linking her hands behind his neck and pressing herself close to him. "Darius, Darius."

"Cygnet." Darius tightened his arms around her. "What is it love?" Concern roughened his voice.

"I . . . I just want you to hold me." She kept her face pressed to him. "Could we go somewhere other than Phil's house for a while? I want to be alone with you."

"I want to be alone with you, too, love." Darius hugged her, then eased her into the passenger seat.

He went around the front of the car, watching her the whole time, and climbed in on his side, firing the engine at once. "I think I know a place where we can walk on the beach with no one to see us but the gulls."

"That's what I want," Cyg whispered, feeling the circle of pain low inside her growing in intensity. She knew with a certainty that made her shiver, that when she was an old woman, the pain would still be with her.

"Cold, love?" Without taking his eyes from the road, Darius reached into the space behind the seats and pulled a lap robe into the front seat. He placed it on Cyg's lap.

Even though she wasn't cold, Cyg spread the robe across her knees murmuring, "Thank you."

They drove in silence for a while, Darius still kissing her hand every so often. They stopped at a deserted beach of barren rock-strewn sand with tussocks of coarse grass dotting the area.

"No one comes here. The riptide is dangerous." He turned to look at her. "Would you like to walk?"

Cyg nodded and lifted the robe from her lap. Darius laughed when he saw her drag the robe from the car and took it from her. He stared out over the expanse of rock and sand, watching the waves rolling in rough cadence to the shore. "I guess there's a few dry spots out on the sand that we can use." He took her hand, leading her down a dirt path through the sea grass to the beach.

They trudged through the sand, listening to the solitude which was broken only by the sounds of their footsteps and the screech of the gulls.

"Here's a sheltered spot." Darius released her hand and spread the blanket on an area below some large boulders. The sun was an orange ball that warmed them; the pile of rocks behind them protected them from the wind.

When Darius lay down beside her, his shirt unbuttoned and pulled free of his trousers, Cyg rolled close to him and put her arms around his neck. Her hands caressed him in nervous need until she felt him sag toward her and scoop her body beneath him.

"Cygnet, my baby swan, you're mine," Darius

muttered into her neck as he nuzzled down her body. "I love your little derriere in those jeans, darling, but I damn well wish you had less of a barricade on today."

"No problem," Cyg said softly, rolling away from him and to her knees. She unbuttoned the shirt to the last button, then let it slide backward off her shoulders. She felt no shyness with Darius even when she heard him catch his breath and mutter her name hoarsely. She rose, her upper torso nude, aware that his eyes were on her and that he was still in the same reclining position. With slow, steady movements, she removed her jeans; her body contracted slightly in the coolness of the day. She was about to slip her bikini pants down when Darius rose in one fluid motion.

"I'll do that, love. Let me." He pulled his shirt from his body and then stripped his jeans downward and kicked them aside along with the jockey shorts he had been wearing. He pulled her to him, letting her feel and see the arousal she had caused.

Loving the feel of him, she closed her eyes as he pulled her to the ground. She felt the beginning roughness of an after midday beard as his face slid down her body, loving her. She heard him laugh deep in his throat when her body arched as the bikini pants were tugged from her body and his kiss deepened in the most intimate way.

Just as he had the first time he loved her, Darius ministered to every part of her body, muttering love words to her over and over again.

"Darius, Darius . . . I love you," Cyg sobbed silently. "I will always belong to you," her mind screamed to him. "This is my good-bye to you, my beloved man." She clung with a ferocity that excited and pleased Darius, making her innate sensuality take fire and erupt over them both.

"My love, my love." Darius's voice had a guttural sound as though he was no longer in control of it.

"Cyg, baby, slow down, you're driving me crazy," he rasped out.

"I don't care." She moaned, writhing beneath him.

"Cygnet, I'll never let you go," Darius breathed as he positioned her body beneath him.

Love erupted like Mauna Loa, Hawaii's famous volcano, pitching them into a love coil that carried them away from all but each other.

Darius soothed her with gentle kisses down her still-shuddering body, bringing the corner of the blanket up to enclose them both. Cyg fell asleep holding him tight, still clasped in his arms.

When she awoke, warm and safe against Darius's chest, the sun was very low in the western sky. She kissed his chest, knowing it was time to go.

"Ummm?" Darius yawned, his chest heaving under Cyg's cheek. "Are you cold, angel?"

"No. Toasty," Cyg crooned, letting her fingers twine in the curling hair on his chest. She didn't want to say anything about going, but she knew she must. "It's late, Darius."

"I know. I just don't feel like going back to that zoo," he said harshly. "I'm glad we'll be leaving tomorrow." He leaned back from her. "Tell your roommate that you won't be going back to New York with her." He gazed down at her, his face solemn. "Tell her I'm driving you back . . . and that you will be moving out of your apartment."

"What are . . . ?"

Darius lay his hand gently over her mouth. "Now don't say anything until you've heard what I have to say. Okay?"

"Okay."

"I want you to move in with me right away. We have a lifetime to plan and I have no intention of doing it over a phone, or picking you up after work and talking then. You belong to me, don't you?"

"I belong to you."

"Well, then, it's all settled." Darius looked away from her as he searched for her clothes. He didn't see her bite her lip until it bled as she fought back the tears. "Now I'll dress you and we'll go back and face that pack of hyenas at Phil's house. Ah, here we are." He held them up in front of him with both hands and shook his head. "You're so damned tiny . . . but I like it, because you have such a nice round bottom."

"Mr. Chadwick . . ." Cyg swallowed, forcing a laugh, ". . . how you talk." She put her arms around his neck, kissing his cheek as he eased the panties up her legs, his hands lingering on her body.

It took them much longer to dress than it had taken them to undress. Laughter punctuated the long kisses as they helped each other with their clothing.

Cyg tried to store away each word, whisper, and nuance. She tried to imprint on her mind every pore on Darius's face. She cursed the moment when she had pawned her camera so that she could buy makeup she needed to go out on a modeling job. Somehow she had never seemed to get enough money together to go and reclaim the camera.

"Hey, lady, you're daydreaming." Darius swept her and the lap robe up into his arms.

"Put me down. I'm too heavy to carry all the way to the car," Cyg protested, loving being held by him.

"You are more solid than you look." Darius laughed, letting her cuff him on the jaw. "But I love having this bundle of bones in my arms."

"Monster," she said in a low tone close to his ear, biting the lobe.

"Ouch!"

"Hurt?" Cyg was gleeful.

"No, but you are having an effect on me. Shall I stop here and begin again?"

Cyg wanted to tell him to stop right there and

make love to her but she knew she had to get back. If she wanted to take the chance and thumb a ride with a truck driver she had better leave before cocktail time. She felt a snake of fear curl in her stomach. She had never hitched a ride with anyone before and didn't like the idea, recalling all the admonitions of her parents while she had been in college. But she had the feeling that the truck route in front of Phil's property would be her only chance to get away quietly.

She held tight to Darius's neck as he walked slowly back to the car. When she began singing a poignant love song, her voice joggling a bit from being carried, it delighted her when Darius murmured, "I love to hear you sing."

The trip back seemed to go too quickly. They talked about everything and anything. Darius told her that he was going to get a box at the Met for her so that she could attend all the operas that she chose.

"You wouldn't like the opera." Cyg smiled weakly.

"I'd like anything where you were." The lopsided heat of his smile felt like another blanket he put over her.

When Cyg saw the entrance to Phil's home, her mouth dried to a desert. She could barely swallow.

"Don't look like that, angel," Darius crooned to her as he drove the car up the drive and parked in the space near the back of the house. "We'll be together all evening. We'll just ignore everyone else."

"Right."

They left the car and walked to the house hand in hand.

Cyg's heart began a slow thudding in her chest as they entered the door and walked toward the stairway. For the first time in her life, she could understand how someone would feel going to their own hanging. She was not going to see Darius again. She would be dead but alive, seeing but blind, hearing but deafened—to everything around her.

Before they parted at her door, Cyg threw her arms around Darius's neck and held him tight, kissing him, her mouth open on his.

"Angel." He groaned. "Don't . . . or I'll be coming in after you. See you later."

" 'Bye Darius."

Dry eyed, Cyg hurried through her small amount of packing, not even bothering to change her clothes. She threw water on her face, cleaned her teeth, picked up her small bag, and left the room, going down the back stairs to the kitchen. She spoke to none of the staff who only paid cursory attention to her. She didn't follow the driveway but walked through the trees edging the drive.

She walked and thumbed and walked.

The third truck that passed her stopped. She stared at the middle-aged man who looked down at her from the cab.

"Need a lift, kid?"

Four

Ever after when Cyg would think about her flight from Phil Tabor's house, she would feel a tinge of horror that she had the nerve to accept a ride from a truck driver. That the truck driver turned out to be a fatherly man with three girls of his own was just a stroke of luck; that he happened to be taking his truck to the market in midtown Manhattan, where he was dropping off some crates before going to northern New York, was a heavenly intervention, Cyg was sure.

It struck Cyg like lightning that that's where she would go. To northern New York! To Aunt Lena in Saratoga Springs! That's where she would go.

"Would it be possible for you to . . ." Cyg gulped breath and looked at Frank Rankin, as the truck driver had introduced himself. ". . . go past my apartment." Cyg rushed her words as she told him about her apartment where she lived with Kim. "You see, since you're going north into the state . . . perhaps near Saratoga . . ."

"Goin' right through it," Frank Rankin answered laconically, the chaw of tobacco in his mouth shifting to his other cheek.

"You are? Oh, that's great. Ah . . . could you . . .

I mean, I could give you a little toward the gas, maybe." Cyg started adding what she would have to give him.

"Just buy me a cup of coffee, kid." Frank turned to smile at her. "I don't like to see kids like you on the road."

Cyg felt such a release from tension that she had to fight tears. "Thank you," she whispered.

Time blurred as she sank into blue thought for the rest of the trip into the city. Once in the apartment, she left a note for Kim telling her that she was leaving. She said good-bye to Mrs. Tonetti asking her to hold all mail until she contacted her.

Cyg felt safe in the truck as it sped through the darkening day and into the long star-clear night. She fell asleep on the Thruway, exhausted by her emotional loss. Darius could never be hers. All she would ever have would be memories.

At one of the truck stops she bought Frank his coffee and called Aunt Lena. Of course she was in bed. Lena Dilson was a trained masseuse at the Roosevelt Baths in Saratoga and she started her day early.

"What? Cyg? Baby, what is it? Are you crying?"

"No," Cyg rasped out, barely able to swallow. "I don't cry. You know that."

"Come on home, love . . . and let me talk to that truck driver."

Cyg didn't want to call Frank to the phone but her aunt was adamant. She watched while he nodded his head into the phone, looked once at her, then handed back the phone, mumbling, "Good lady."

They got to her aunt's house at two o'clock in the morning. Aunt Lena insisted that Frank come in for a breakfast of eggs and sausage that she had prepared. After Frank left, Cyg talked to her aunt for a short time, and it was four in the morning before she climbed between the sweet-smelling percale sheets.

Cyg slept until noon, waking with a muzzy headache that throbbed over her right eye. "I never get headaches," she grumbled, staggering into the bathroom across the hall from her room, one hand pressing against the ache in her forehead. "I refuse to allow you to give me headaches, Darius Chadwick. I *can* live without you," she muttered as she turned her face up to the stream of hot water in the shower. "I will not be depressed either." She toweled herself so hard that her skin tingled to a rosy pink color.

Donning jeans and a rolled-neck pullover in the same gold color as the stitching in the jeans, and a shade deeper than her eyes, she hopped down the stairs two at a time. She had an appetite, she had an appetite, she gritted to herself over and over as she read Aunt Lena's note telling her to help herself to breakfast, then to walk or take the bicycle in the garage over to the baths.

Cyg determinedly chewed every mouthful of wheat cereal with sliced bananas, noting on the box that there was no salt or sugar or artificial ingredients. Aunt Lena was still a pure food freak, Cyg thought, smiling as she sipped at the herbal tea. Aunt Lena didn't allow caffeine products in the house.

After cleaning up the kitchen, straightening her room and unpacking her few things, she went out in back to look at the bike. It was in good condition, even though it was as modern as the Ark. Balloon tires and a cushioned saddle seat set the vintage about 1935, Cyg figured.

It took Cyg a few minutes to figure out that if she wanted to move the action was strictly up to her. No gears to ease the way! It was pump, pump the old legs.

She headed down her aunt's street, weaving just a bit as she tried to get the feel of the Model A bicycle. Birch Street was narrow with no sidewalks, but there was also very little traffic.

When she came to the main thoroughfare that would take her to the Gideon Putnam Hotel, then beyond it to the Roosevelt Baths, she was puffing like a steam engine. The ride through the park-like area was as beautiful as she remembered it being when she was younger. She saw other people on bikes, ten-speeds of course, but she waved to them and shouted "Hi" when they passed her, as they did to her.

She was feeling quite confident in her ability when she looked up and saw a silver Ferrari in the traffic ahead. Her bike wobbled and she almost fell. When she looked again it was gone. Impossible! If she would stop thinking of the man, the bogeys would go away. Where was her pride? Darius Chadwick thought of her as a call girl. He had even told her that he owed Phil money that one day, but he hadn't wanted to explain why. She knew. Cyg pedaled faster, trying to outrun her thoughts.

When she finally reached the Gideon she didn't stop to admire the beautiful brick building with the circular drive and the white portico. Instead, she biked onward like a fury through the trees to the temporary haven of the Roosevelt Baths. Reason told her that Darius wasn't in Saratoga, that it was not his Ferrari, but panic told her to hide. She locked her bike and ran into the low brick structure, out of breath by the time she reached the reception area. "I'll need a good soak and a massage myself." Cyg groaned as she took deep breaths in front of the desk before asking for Lena Dilson.

"Do you have an appointment?" The thick lenses on the woman's glasses caught the sun from the doorway and gave her the look of an owl.

"No. I'm her niece."

"Oh. Do you have an appointment?"

"Oh, well, you see Aunt Lena asked me . . ."

"There you are Cyg, dear," Aunt Lena caroled. Her voice sounded hollow in the tile-lined reception area. "Have you met Claudia Dill? No? Claudia, this is Cyg Melton, my niece."

"Does she have an appointment?"

Aunt Lena pursed her lips. "No, she doesn't have an appointment."

"Then she can't have a massage." Claudia's glasses sent prisms of light dancing over the maroon, tan, and green tiles of the reception area.

Aunt Lena bent down and removed Claudia's glasses, set them carefully on the desk, and took hold of the woman's shoulders. Claudia blinked upward. "My niece is coming here for a job interview with Wentworth."

"Oh." Claudia fumbled on the desk, her hands searching crab-like for her glasses. "Wentworth will see her now."

"Thank you." Aunt Lena exhaled, placing the hornrimmed glasses into Claudia's hand, and grabbed Cyg's arms and pulled her along the corridor to a room marked OFFICE.

Wentworth was an ageless gorgon of a man, baldheaded and muscular, with a face like an Easter Island carving.

In two minutes, Cyg discovered he was gentle and dedicated to the maxim MENTAL HEALTH THROUGH PHYSICAL WELL-BEING, which was on a sign over his desk. During the forty-minute interview, he pointed to it several times. When she was told that she could report tomorrow and that she would be apprenticed to a woman called only Marianne, Cyg nearly loosened his arm from its socket, she shook his hand so hard.

Cyg spent the next three hours following her aunt around the baths, trying to familiarize herself with the procedures. Her aunt promised her that she would give Cyg her first bath and massage at the Roosevelt Baths the very next day.

"But I'm sure I went to the baths when I was younger, Aunt Lena." Cyg frowned trying to remember.

"Lincoln Baths." Aunt Lena pronounced, stretching her neck in a door and assuring a Mrs. Greeb that she was just fine and that, to her knowledge, no one had ever drowned in the Roosevelt Baths.

"Oh, yes, I remember now. They were more downtown."

"Right. Now, Cyg, I want you to stop by the Gideon and pick up some vegetables from Silvers. He's one of the bellhops." Aunt Lena stormed down the halls, Cyg trotting at her heels. "Man's a genius in that hot house of his. Grows all sorts of things. Still, he won't retire from the Gideon. Likes it too much."

"How will I know him?" Cyg panted after her aunt as she stopped at other rooms and spoke to the guests taking the waters.

Aunt Lena stopped so suddenly that Cyg plowed into her. "Pull yourself together, girl. Ask at the desk. I left instructions on the table for our meal. Follow 'em." Aunt Lena flapped her hand in farewell.

Cyg wrestled her bike back along the path to the Gideon, welcoming the sun on her face. It was going to be a lovely day.

When she arrived in front of the Gideon, she put her bike in the stand and locked it. Then she looked up at the beautiful building with its rose-hued bricks and white portico glistening jewel-like in the sun. She gasped; there was that silver Ferrari again.

She took a deep breath and scurried after a uniformed bellboy into the spacious, white pillared lobby. To the left was a small card and novelty shop, to the right was the desk, straight ahead was a large lounging area for guests. Beyond that through glass doors was a solarium-type room where a buffet-type meal was still being served.

Cyg stepped to the desk and cleared her throat. A man not much older than herself, lifted his head and smiled at her. "My name is Cygnet Melton and I'm to see a gentleman called Mr. Silvers . . ."

"Just Silvers," the youngish man with the slicked blond hair informed her gently.

"Oh. Well, is Just Silvers in?"

The smile disappeared from the blond man's face. "His name is Silvers . . . not Mr. Silvers, or anything else."

"Gotcha," Cyg whispered. "May I speak to him?"

The blond man inhaled, leaned back to look at the wall next to him, and then pressed a hidden buzzer. He went back to studying the papers in front of him.

Silvers was a medium-sized man, medium bald, medium old with a Beagle Hound look to him even when he smiled. "You must be Lena's niece from New York . . . the model."

"Sometimes I was a model." Cyg smiled as she followed him through some swinging doors to a storage area. "Sometimes I work part-time as a physiotherapist."

Silvers's laugh sounded like a hoot. "Like Aunt, like niece eh?" He leaned down, picked up a bag and handed it to her. "There's green beans and tomatoes and onions in there . . . Added some lettuce, too."

"Thank you . . . ah . . . Silvers."

"Welcome." His eyelids seemed to slide over his eyes and not rise again. "Workin'?"

Cyg grinned at him. "I have a part-time job at the baths. I just got it a few minutes ago. Of course, I'd like more time . . ." Cyg shrugged.

Silvers pursed his lips. "Come with me. I heard that Legg is leaving. That's the fellow on the desk when you came in. They just shifted him to night clerk so he quit . . . that's what I heard. Let me talk to Minnie Brown. She's the housekeeper and she knows when the Gideon breathes." He ushered Cyg into a tiny office where a heavy set woman was standing in front of a file drawer.

Cyg was introduced to Minnie, who in turn introduced her to the assistant manager.

When Cyg walked out of the Gideon by a side door Minnie showed her, she carried the vegetables to her bike, in a happy daze. She would be working at the Gideon four nights a week as a desk clerk.

As she made her way back down the winding parklike road to route 50 that would take her back to Birch Street, Cyg promised herself that she would make Aunt Lena take board from her or she wouldn't stay. Now that she had two salaries coming in, she could well afford to pay for her keep and she would insist on doing so.

A car honked at her as it went by, the man shaking his fist at her and yelling at her to get over to the side of the road. She thought she saw the Ferrari again and she closed her eyes for a moment. When she opened them, the car was gone. Imagination!

"Same to you, fella," Cyg shouted, feeling too jubilant to be really angry. Besides, she had to admit the man had a point: Her erratic handling of the bike could stand improvement.

When she reached Birch Street and Aunt Lena's small house, Cyg was so hot and sweaty that the first thing she did was to take a shower and change into a cotton denim skirt and a cotton plaid shirt. Summer was coming to northern New York at last.

Hopping down the stairs again to the kitchen, Cyg donned a Hoover apron and began to read the instructions that Aunt Lena had left for chicken teriyaki done on the grill.

Rummaging through the freezer in the summer kitchen, she found many frozen pies her aunt had put up. She decided on apple, preheated the oven and started the pie.

After dinner was started, she vacuumed the downstairs and congratulated herself on how well her life was working out. When a voice deep inside her mentioned Darius, she smothered it with more work. She would survive.

The baths and the Gideon Putnam Hotel swelled with patrons and guests. Cyg liked both jobs because she met interesting people, but she had to admit that she got a greater satisfaction from working at the baths, especially when there was an opportunity to really help someone by giving a massage. The people with arthritis, who had palpable relief from pain after one of her treatments, made Cyg feel very good.

Maura Tiebold was one of those persons. She wasn't really old, still in her sixties, but Aunt Lena had said that sometimes the woman's pain was acute.

Cyg walked into the private room where Mrs. Tiebold was immersed in one of the huge rectangular tubs. "Have you fallen asleep on me?" Cyg leaned over the older woman, whose chin was resting on a towel.

"No, Cyg, dear." Mrs. Tiebold's eyes fluttered open. "But I feel I could fall asleep here. It feels so good to be suspended in hot bubbling water."

"Doesn't it?" Cyg laughed and helped the woman to her feet. Then she wrapped her in a towel and assisted her out of the bath. "Why do you think I would like Aunt Lena to massage me if I had the time?"

Maura Tiebold gave Cyg, who was standing beside the older woman, a narrow-eyed look. She was dressed in nurse's white, her blond curls piled on top of her head. "You look as though you should be in a fashion magazine, child, not giving elderly women back rubs."

Cyg chuckled as she edged the woman onto the

gurney-type stretcher bed that she used for massages. She locked the wheels, then lifted the sheet back from Mrs. Tiebold's body. In the short time she had worked with the woman, Cyg had come to know the special pressure points that needed attention first.

"You know, my dear, that first day, when you took over for Lena, I wasn't sure that you would be able to do the job." The woman sighed as Cyg jerked her toes and stretched her foot. "But now I ask for you all the time. Of course I still think Lena is wonderful, but you do have the most marvelous hands." Maura paused. "And of course, Marianne is very good . . . even if she doesn't look as though she could do anything." Maura chuckled sleepily.

"Marianne fools everyone. The first time I saw her, when my training started here, I thought, that poor, fragile, frail old lady couldn't do a toe pull. What a surprise! She gave me a massage that first week. It was like a six-months' crash course in how to give body rubs. She's marvelous."

"But forgetful." Maura yawned.

"Oh, you mustn't think that leaving someone in the waters for forty minutes is normal with her. It was just horrendously busy that day."

"I understand Hortense Davis looked like a plump dried apricot, color and all." Maura was half asleep.

"Yes." Cyg bit her lips to keep from laughing as she remembered how it had taken both she and Lena to get the woman out of the tub. Hortense's body was so flaccid she couldn't make a fist, let alone grip the sides of the tub and lift herself out. She had slept through her entire massage and for an hour thereafter. Each time she had come to the baths since then, she had tried to talk any attendant that she might have into leaving her in the baths again. She informed anyone who would listen that she had slept for twenty-four hours and hadn't had insomnia since. To Hortense Davis, the baths were a cure-all!

Cyg kept moving from guest to guest, feeling a good tiredness in her body, grateful for the physical concentration of her job that allowed her on most nights to fall into bed and sleep dreamlessly until dawn. For some reason that she didn't try to fathom, Cyg was unable to sleep past the rising of the sun. As she rose at six anyway, that hour was the one when the pain of losing Darius Chadwick seemed to expand until she was left gasping at the enormity of her hurt. In that dawn hour even her fingernails were numb, as if they had just been dealt a sharp blow. Her toes would curl into the sheets and blankets covering her in the dormer room she occupied on the second floor of her aunt's house. When she dozed one morning at five and woke to the sound of her own groaning, she was glad that her aunt slept in the bedroom on the first floor. Darius, Darius, Darius. The name sang in her mind like the pulse of her blood. Reason told her that the loss would be less tearing with time. She clung to the belief that he thought of her as being a call girl and that he could never really love her feeling that way.

She said good-bye to each of her patrons personally, enjoying the few minutes she had with each one before they left. Since Maura Tiebold was one of her favorites she tried to take a little longer with her.

"And do you go right from here to your job at the Gideon, dear?" Maura inquired, nodding to her handyman who had come to fetch her in the ancient Rolls Royce brougham that was in mint condition and had not a particle of dust on its gleaming surface. The back seat was like a small room, Cyg thought as she helped Mrs. Tiebold into the car.

"Yes. Usually I get over to the Gideon in time to

have dinner. The food is so good. I look forward to it." Cyg smiled at Maura.

"Wise girl. I generally try to get to the Gideon once a week myself whenever I have friends staying there. Lovely place." Maura frowned. "Not that you look any fatter than when you first arrived." She nodded to her chauffeur. "And those shadows are still in your eyes my dear." Maura's voice faded as the window slid up the into place.

Cyg looked after the car for a long time. I'm doing my best to forget him, she told herself, as she went back into the baths.

She took time to talk to Aunt Lena before she left for the short walk to the Gideon.

"Cyg, I wish you would take my car. I worry about you pedaling that bike home after midnight," Lena complained as she folded linens and put them into neat piles for the morning.

"Auntie . . ." Cyg leaned over and kissed her aunt. "You worry too much. I'll be just fine and I find that the bike ride home relaxes me." Cyg didn't say she needed the extra exertion to help her sleep.

"There are dangerous people around, even in Saratoga, my dear."

"Yes, but they couldn't catch me on Old Nuts and Bolts. Now that I have that infernal machine figured out, it is a positive giant on the road."

Cyg said good-bye to her aunt and promised her that she would be careful pedaling home.

Cyg stood in the shade of a majestic maple and inhaled the warm sweet air. Tonight when her shift ended she would be riding home in the coolness of the evening, the atmosphere scented with the bloom of flowers. Then she saw the Ferrari parked on the circular drive.

She smiled at Steve, the day clerk, not really seeing him, and listened to all the special messages that had not yet been passed to the various guests.

"Will you be coming to the Arts Center on Saturday to watch the New York ballet company?" Steve asked her.

Cyg felt a buzzing in her ears when she shook her head no. She wanted to hide. Steve was getting too close. She didn't want that either. She couldn't handle that. Neither could she handle thinking that she saw Darius behind every tree and every bush. "No, I have to work Saturday night." Cyg tried to put some regret in her voice.

"Lord, it will be a madhouse Saturday." Steve grimaced. "Not only will you miss the ballet, but you will also be handling a flood of guests coming in. I understand that one of the biggies has leased his suite for the entire month of August."

"Then why would he be coming the last week in July?"

Steve shrugged. "Who knows? Maybe he wants to be settled in by the time the racing starts on July twenty-eighth. Who can figure the rich?"

Cyg laughed, but didn't encourage him to stay. She had plenty to do getting in touch with guests and giving them their messages, answering the switchboard and speaking with patrons who came to the desk.

The evening flew by. There was no mad rush, but there was steady work to fill her mind until ten-thirty rolled around. She had a short shift tonight and she was glad. She had a feeling that she would sleep that night and she was right. She slept right through until five in the morning, then wrestled and tossed with thoughts of Darius until it was time to rise and shower again.

She didn't have to work at the Gideon that evening, so when Steve Marwell called and asked her if she wanted to go down to the racetrack to watch a few preliminary races, Cyg accepted at once. She had always loved watching the thoroughbreds run and it had been a long time since she had been to her parents' farm. She thought it would seem like home to watch the high-strung beauties go through their paces.

She dressed in cotton dress jeans in a champagne color with a matching silk shirt in the same shade that was just a hue lighter than her eyes.

"I like that shirt, honey," Aunt Lena said.

"It's three years old." Cyg grinned at her relative. "I bought it when I was doing the stocking commercials. I was making money then, so I indulged myself."

"Good things stand the test of time," Aunt Lena remarked, nodding her head, her half glasses bobbing on her nose.

There was a rap on the screen door. Before Lena could rise, Cyg went to answer it, letting Steve in and taking him into the living room.

"Hello, Steve. How are you? Still in that summer course you were taking?" Aunt Lena looked over her glasses.

"I'll be done in three weeks." Steve rolled his eyes. "I must have been crazy to take it."

"It will cut down on some of your master's course time, won't it?" Cyg asked, tying the sleeves of a cotton sweater around her neck. The light cinnamon color suited her jeans and shirt. "Good night Aunt Lena." Cyg kissed her cheek.

"Yes . . . but it cuts into my social life, too. Good night Mrs. Dilson."

Steve was a good companion and he, like Cyg, had grown up with horses. "Of course with me, it was being raised so close to the Saratoga track. I don't know how many tons of manure I've forked in my time."

They walked to the track enjoying the summer evening.

"Me, too." Cyg laughed. "My dad told me if I

wanted to be with the horses I would have to do my share of the work."

"How long were you low man on the totem pole?" Steve asked.

"I never seemed to rise above stable swamper." Cyg chuckled. "It's a good thing I loved those horses."

"Yeah, it helps."

She and Steve wandered onto the track grounds, moving slowly and watching as the small crowd of people bought tickets and went through the tunnels under the bleachers. Before they went through she had a fleeting panicking moment when she saw a silver Ferrari. She shook off the panic. Many summer visitors in Saratoga drove such cars.

The track's center was a garden of summer flowers, the colors crossing the spectrum with every tint and hue.

"There are as many colors of silks as there are flowers here," Steve mused leaning on the track rail.

"It even smells successful." Cyg lifted her shoulders as Steve stared at her. "You know. It doesn't have that ordinary stable smell. The odor is . . . richer."

"You're a crazy lady, Cyg. Manure is manure, whether it's a plow horse or a racer."

"Blasphemy," Cyg whispered, her nostrils flaring as she inhaled the atmosphere of Saratoga.

"William Travers, whose name is on one of the famous races here must be turning in his grave." Steve scowled at her. "I'm not sure that it isn't dangerous for me to be with you. You might be a reincarnation of one of those good old boys that started the Saratoga Association for the Improvement of the Breed."

"Serve you right if I was." Cyg laughed.

"Will you be coming to any of the races, Cyg?"

"Probably not. Even if I have the time off, I don't suppose I could get near the rail."

"I think I'll come for one, even if I do end up trampled to death. I . . ." Steve continued to speak to her as he turned her toward the grandstand, but Cyg didn't hear.

Up there through the glass enclosure of the VIP lounge she saw a wraith. It had to be a wraith. The late-day sun double refracted off the glasses of the wraith standing looking down at them.

Darius . . . Darius, her mind screamed. It can't be you, it isn't you. You can't be here. You must despise call girls. I wasn't fooled by your tenderness, she shrieked at him in her mind as he stood there looking too solid for a ghost. You don't know me, her brain yelled at him, and I won't explain that I am not what you thought. Go away. Leave me . . .

". . . still get a big boot out of watching those babies crash out of the gate and pound over the turf. Don't you?"

"Yes," the automaton Cyg pronounced, letting him lead her to one of the seats in the grandstand. She didn't look at the VIP section. She forced Darius Chadwick from her mind. Her life was going to progress . . . without gloom . . . without depression.

She let her great love for the thoroughbreds fill her mind. She picked her choice to win. Standing, she cheered and shouted him home. Her horse came in third but it in no way lessened her enjoyment of the preliminary races.

"Bringing you to a sporting event could be dangerous." Steve grinned. "If I wasn't a naturally fast man at ducking, I would have been decapitated more than once."

Cyg poked her tongue at him. "Fool. You can only be decapitated once." Her spirits lifted as common sense convinced her that she couldn't have seen Darius.

"Oh, God, I'm dating an intellectual." Steve flinched most convincingly when Cyg punched him in the arm.

It had been years since Cyg had been to an ice cream shop and had a real honest-to-goodness chocolate soda. Steve took her to a real old-fashioned shop. The soda fountain had round red-and-white ruffled stools. There were tiny round tables with red-and-white cloths and cushions on the wire-backed chair seats.

She and Steve sat at the fountain. When Cyg saw the tall frothy glass set in front of her, her mouth began to water. "Oh, lovely." She sighed as she pulled at the straw. "Aren't they just heaven?"

Steve shrugged, drank some of his and nodded. "It's good, but I still prefer a cold beer."

"Plebeian," Cyg hissed at him from the side of her mouth, looking lovingly at her chocolate soda glass and its dwindling contents.

The walk home was through soft velvet air, the spicy smell of pinks from a garden perfuming their way. Cyg felt stronger every minute.

"Saratoga is a lovely place."

"When you're with the right girl," Steve said and placed his hand at her waist.

Cyg moved slightly away from his hand and Steve let it drop, saying nothing. "Steve . . . I really enjoyed tonight, but I'm not ready for anything more than friendship."

"Somebody stepped on you, huh?"

"Something like that." Cyg turned to look at him, then slipped her hand through his arm. "I have really had a good evening, the best since I got here."

"Good. We'll work on that."

They parted that night with a handshake and a promise on Cyg's part that she would most certainly like to go swimming with him up at Lake George on her first day off.

The next day was a long and grueling one at the baths. She assisted Marianne with several arthritic patients who came regularly to the baths and the strain of lifting some of them, the ones who were virtually helpless in getting in and out of the tubs, stretched her muscles to the aching point. When she was finished, she stared in awe at Marianne who preceded her down the tiled corridor, seemingly as untired now as she had been that morning, shuffling along in crepe-soled white shoes that looked more like barges than footwear. Marianne's secret to good feet, according to her, was to wear shoes at least two sizes too large. It gave her swelling feet room to expand, but of course she was unable to spring her foot because the shoe would come off, hence the shuffling gait. Aunt Lena often commented that hearing Marianne come down the tiled hall was like listening to Frankenstein approach.

A woman came forward from the desk as she and Marianne entered the reception area.

She pressed money into Marianne's hand. "I'm Mrs. Jan Tharp . . . I was here yesterday." The attractive ash-blonde woman elaborated as Marianne looked at her blankly. "I just had to return and tell you that my back has never felt better and I danced last night and everything. Thank you." Mrs. Tharp smiled at Cyg as well, then turned and left the building.

"Well, I guess I'll buy some vegetables from Silvers with this. I think a spinach salad sounds dandy. See you tomorrow Cyg." Marianne shuffled down the hall to get her handbag.

"Don't you ever get tired?" Cyg muttered after the retreating woman, who was moving at the same slow speed she had started with that morning.

"Do you have an appointment?" The owl-eyed Claudia looked in Cyg's direction. "You can't get a massage without an appointment."

Cyg watched sun rays refract off Claudia's glasses for a moment. "Right." She sighed and followed the same path Marianne had taken to the employees' locker rooms. It was going to be a tough evening at the Gideon, Cyg mused, smothering a yawn with one hand.

As soon as she arrived at the hotel employees' entrance, Silvers waved her over to a corner of the kitchen. "Tonight one of the entrées is lemon sole. I have a nice piece for you and some lovely marinated zucchini and tomatoes from my own garden. So good. Sit down right here. You look tired."

"Ummmm, it looks and smells marvelous." Cyg took a deep breath. "I'm tired, Silvers. Marianne and I had some of the arthritics from the Hilton Home. Some of them are heavy, but it makes me happy to know that some of them leave the Roosevelt Baths feeling much, much better than when they arrived." Cyg forked the tender fish into her mouth and appreciated the piquancy the soupçon of lemon had added to the taste. "This is so good." She savored the fresh vegetables which had been marinated in vinegar, black pepper, a little oil, and some brown sugar, under Silver's watchful eye.

He refilled her glass of skimmed milk twice, muttering that she should be drinking whole Guernsey milk to fatten her up.

"I heard that. Between you and Aunt Lena, I'll be as big as a house." Cyg sighed, pushed back her plate and shook her head when Silvers was going to fill it up again. "No more. I couldn't."

"Now wait. Rene has something special tonight." Silvers wagged his index finger at her.

"No . . . no desert. I won't be able to move," Cyg complained, then was still when she saw the homemade chocolate éclair. "Oh Lord, a chocoholic's delight. That topping must be an inch thick. I'm going to die like Attila the Hun, by overindulging myself." She groaned, closing her eyes as she lifted her fork again.

After repairing her makeup in the ladies' room, Cyg tottered to the desk. She was angry with herself for eating the éclair but also knew that she wouldn't be able to resist describing it to her Aunt Lena, who also had a fatal weakness for desserts, especially chocolate.

To Cyg's surprise, the traffic coming into the Gideon increased after seven o'clock. It seemed that many of the guests wanted to be settled in their rooms days before the actual racing began.

Cyg wasn't even flustered when she looked up and saw several of the baggage caddies waiting in the lobby, people milling around the desk, giving her inquiring looks.

She managed to placate Mr. Hoover who was upset that he didn't get Room 205.

"Miss, I have had that room for three seasons. I'm used to the bed." Mrs. Hoover nodded over her husband's shoulder, her birdlike features quivering with feeling.

"Mr. Hoover, if there is any question of you being uncomfortable in Room 320, it will be changed at once." Cyg smiled. "I do believe the mattresses on the third floor are all new. So, if you'd like to try it . . ." Cyg let her voice trail off as she watched the two elderly people huddle over the question. She tried not to look at the growing crowd in the background.

Mr. Hoover turned around and smiled. "We'll try Room 320."

Cyg exhaled and signaled to Silvers to take the baggage to the third floor. "Good evening, sir. May I help you?"

And on it went until Cyg was sure that they must have given out every room in the hotel.

She reached the point where she didn't even raise her head after greeting each of the guests. That way she seemed to be able to move them more rapidly.

Others, like the Hoovers, caviled at the rooms they were assigned, but most times, Cyg was able to smooth things over and keep calm.

She was congratulating herself on her progress

as the number of guests gathered in front of the desk lessened. She had climbed her Mount Everest for the day and was beginning the slide down.

Perhaps it was a tad too early to breathe a sigh of relief, but Cyg did it anyway. Right after she finished with Mr. Waite and "traveling companion," she leaned back, arching her back and rubbing her forehead.

"I'll bet you're ready for a break," said David Deering her alternate, who had been called in to help her.

"Yes, but unless my eyes deceive me, the witching hour is here and you and I can close the window for the night." Cyg tried to smother a yawn behind her hand.

When she heard the rustle of movement and the squeak of the baggage caddy near the entrance, she groaned. When David lifted her out of the chair and urged her toward a side chair near the telephone console, she sank into it gratefully, glad that David was taking her place for the last of the registering guests for that evening.

"Good evening. I'm Darius Chadwick. I think you have a reservation for me."

"Of course, sir," David replied in his most courteous Gideon Putnam voice, not even noticing that Cyg was sliding off her chair to the floor, trying to hide.

Five

Cyg was never too sure how she managed to ride Old Nuts and Bolts home that night. She must have been on automatic pilot. She didn't give a thought to safety or caution and it was a blessing that the headlight and reflectors on the bike were good.

When Lena spoke to her as she stepped into the house, she merely shook her head and turned like a somnambulist toward the stairs.

She lay on her back on the bed, her arms stiff at her sides, staring up at the dark ceiling. He wasn't a wraith! He was here! Her aunt walked into the room and flicked on the lights.

"Cyg? Cyg, look at me. You are going to drink this herb tea. And don't try to tell me it's too hot for herb tea. There's something wrong and if you don't want to tell me, you needn't. It's as if you have a mild case of shock, Cyg. You've got to break that spell you're in . . . and right now."

Cyg responded to the worry in her aunt's voice, inching herself up on her elbows until she was sitting against the high, carved mahogany headboard of the bed. "He's here." Cyg pushed the words past lips as stiff as cardboard; her voice was scratchy as a nail drawn down a blackboard.

"I thought at first it was my imagination when I saw him."

Lena stared at her, her faded blue eyes pinning Cyg's. "You're pale." Lena inhaled sharply. "*He* is the reason you were running? Why you came to Saratoga?"

"Yes." Cyg's hands were shaking so badly that Lena had to hold the mug with the tea.

"Has he hurt you?"

"He beat me to death with love." Cyg felt as if her face were collapsing like a punctured tube. "That was a stupid thing to say."

"Yes, since it paints a horrible picture." Lena took Cyg's cold hand in both of hers and chafed it. "Silly of you to be cold on such a warm night."

"Very silly."

"Did he tell you that he didn't love you?"

"No. He said that he wanted to plan a lifetime with me." Cyg bit hard on her lower lip.

"Oh."

"He thinks I'm a call girl," she said solemnly.

"Good Lord! I shall straighten that young man out in a hurry." Lena seemed to swell with outrage.

"He's not a young man . . ." Cyg swallowed. "Well, I mean, he's not old." She fastened a shaking hand to her mouth. "I don't know how old he is . . . or what he does for a living. Kim said he has money." She sucked in air. "He's probably a cat burglar."

Lena seemed to sort her disjointed conversation and put it in order. "You're in love with him."

"Yes. It's awful. Love makes you sick."

"True. It can also make you very, very well." Lena rose abruptly and left the room.

Cyg could hear the water running in the tiny bathroom across the hall from her room.

Lena came back with a wet cloth that she placed on Cyg's forehead. "You are not going to die."

"I know that," Cyg mumbled, pushing at the cloth on her face as some of the moisture leaked down her cheek.

"Don't interrupt. I was saying, you won't die. Neither will you go into an old-fashioned decline. That was considered de rigeur in my grandmother's day, but, I will try to do my part by being a buffer for you when I can."

Cyg lifted the corner of the cloth so that she could look at her aunt. "I love you, Lena Dilson. You must have been a terror when you were at Skidmore."

"Likewise. And I was." Lena kissed her, removed the cloth, wiped her face with a dry towel, and left the room.

Cyg didn't expect to sleep. She slept from exhaustion. She woke at the usual time and the thoughts of Darius surfaced at once. Each moment of the time they spent together seemed to balloon in kaleidoscopic clarity. Cyg was sure she could remember the exact number of pores on his face, the position of each bristle on that shaven face. "Darius, if I could paint, I would do it now. Better yet, I wish I was a sculptor. I'd carve you in natural teak, all your muscles, your six-foot-two, or is it three-inch frame, your gorgeous hair that is brown with red lights sometimes and red with brown lights other times. I would show the arrow of hair on your chest that is a shade deeper than on your head. Your long tapering hands that look as though you play the piano . . . Do you play the piano?" Cyg was surprised when her hand wiped wetness from her cheek. She never cried. "Darius, were you a football player? I heard Phil say that you boxed in college. How long ago was that? I know your suits come from the best tailors and your shoes are handmade. Did you know how sexy you look in faded jeans and scuffed sneakers? Darius, I know you eat caviar the way I eat peanut butter, but did you know how gorgeous you look with a dot of yellow mustard on your chin?" Cyg groaned and turned over, pushing her face into the pillow, knowing she couldn't hide from her thoughts.

She must have dozed off, because when she woke the house was very silent. She showered and changed into clean jeans, folding her fresh white uniform into her knapsack along with the two oranges that would be her lunch. She read the note from Lena telling her to take the day off . . . to call her at the baths and she would explain to Wentworth.

Cyg had no intention of taking the day off.

Pedaling to the baths was the exertion that she needed to abrade the rough edges of her emotions. She even managed to shake her fist at a motorist who had come too close to her as she rode the bike path toward the baths, but she almost fell when she saw a silver car in the traffic.

As usual, Claudia was already at the desk. "I'm sorry there is no massage without an appointment," she intoned.

Cyg was too tired to ask the woman what it was she really saw through her glasses; she was just too weak to tackle her that morning. "Hi, Claudia."

To her great satisfaction, her day was full enough to drive almost all thoughts of Darius from her head.

By the time Maura Tiebold came for her appointment, Cyg was almost on an even keel.

"You look happy today, Mrs. Tiebold," Cyg observed, smiling at the woman who lay in the effervescent waters. She reached down to give Maura a hand sitting up, then rising. Cyg was quick to wrap the warmed sheet around the woman's delicate body.

"I am. My nephew is staying with me and he is always the most entertaining of all my visitors." Maura gave her an impish smile. "He's a bit of a devil, but he's still the same sweet boy he's always been. I told him about you . . . and for the first time he seemed interested in the baths."

"I can't give him a massage." Cyg grinned. "If

he's tall enough, he can pretend he's a grown-up and go on the men's side."

Maura chuckled. "Oh, he's tall enough, I think."

"Good," Cyg answered. "Then you must bring him with you sometime. Do his parents let him stay with you during the summer?"

"His parents never paid too much attention to what he did . . . at any time." Maura was lying on her stomach and her face was turned to one side as she spoke.

Cyg noticed the tightening of the woman's mouth. "A bit neglected was he?" she asked as she massaged the calf muscle on the left leg.

"More than a bit," Maura said, her voice grim.

"Then he must have loved to come to Saratoga." Cyg thought of the small boy coming into the home of the lovely warm woman she was ministering to. "I suppose he loves to go to the races." Cyg eased her onto her side and began to knead the hip joint under her hands. When Maura Tiebold sighed with relief, Cyg smiled. That was what made the job so worthwhile, knowing that someone was getting palpable results at her hands.

"Cyg," Maura exhaled a deep breath. "Could you come to lunch with Lena . . . on Thursday?"

Cyg bit her lips, running her schedule by her mind's eye. Thursday was going to be a short day at the baths. She would finish Mrs. Dade at eleven and she didn't have to be at the Gideon until seven. "Yes, I could come with Aunt Lena that day."

"Good. I want you to meet my nephew. Is twelve-thirty all right with you?"

"Fine. I'll bring clothes to the baths, then Aunt Lena can pick me up here. Thursday is her day off."

"S'what she told me," Maura muttered sinking into the euphoria that usually followed the baths and a massage.

Cyg never ceased to wonder at the salubrious effects of the effervescent waters of the spa.

She left Maura sleeping, her face calm and

serene, and went to check on her other patrons. In the hall she saw her aunt coming out of one of the bath cubicles. "Hi. Mrs. Tiebold invited me to join you for lunch on Thursday. Will it be a hassle for you to come by here and pick me up in the car?"

"Not at all." Her aunt put her hand on Cyg's arm. "I like to see you get out . . . forget things for a little while."

Cyg kissed her aunt on the cheek, then jogged to the cubicle where a woman was shouting that she had lost all feeling in her arms. Since Cyg knew that first timers at the bath were often appalled at the enervating effects of the waters, she hurried to reassure the woman and explain about the total relaxation of the muscles.

Thursday turned out to be a dreadful day. Nothing went right. The clean linens were misplaced. Instead of one or two first timers, Cyg had four. They were friends and kept shouting to one another or asking Cyg to take messages back and forth between cubicles.

Cyg felt like a dishrag as she showered and changed in the employees' bath. She had brought along a cotton sundress in a deep gold color that did much to emphasize her hair and eyes, making them take on a honey-hued sheen. The thin straps served to delineate the light tan she had acquired on the two separate days she and Steve had gone to Lake George to swim. She wore sandals in a natural calf and carried a matching calf bag. These two items were from her days as the "stocking commercial girl" and though they were three years old they were still stylish. The two-inch heels made her an even five foot ten inches tall and made her slender build appear fragile.

Feeling relaxed, she met her aunt outside the baths at a quarter past twelve.

"You look good today, Cyg. I like your hair free

and flowing. All those wheat blond curls tumbling down your back that way! What hair you have, child!" Her aunt put the aging Pinto with the rusting doors in first gear with a decided jerk, then they coasted down the drive to the larger road which would take them out of the park.

The drive to Maura Tiebold's house was not a long one. She lived on the other side of town in one of the stately houses within walking distance of Skidmore College.

Cyg took a deep breath and rested her head against the back of the seat.

"Rough morning?"

"Four first timers . . . screeching at one another, wanting constant attention. I felt like a teacher at a water-type kindergarten."

Lena laughed, nodding her head. "I know the type. This time of year you get them all."

Cyg stared at the gracious buildings of Skidmore College. "Both you and Mom went there, didn't you?"

"Yep. This is where I introduced my brother to your mother. Love at third sight, I think. They fought too much the first few times they were together."

Cyg laughed. "That's what Mom says. Dad says that he just listened while Mom chewed him out about everything under the sun."

"That'll be the day when your father lets anyone chew him out without going back at them." Lena spoke of her brother with sharp affection, making Cyg laugh again.

Both she and Lena ahhhed with delight as the Pinto grunted up the curved stone drive to the old brick two-story home with the half-circle portico. All the trim on the home was white including the three dormers on the third floor. The front door stood open like welcoming arms as they parked under the portico.

Maura Tiebold was on the top step as Cyg and

her aunt alighted from the car. "I never worry about flies or insects in the house. I keep a very well-trained toad in the garden," Maura told them, a glitter of laughter in her eyes.

"I have one too, plus a very hungry praying mantis," Aunt Lena said firmly, taking hold of Maura's outstretched hand.

"Yes, he is a hungry one." Cyg smiled at Maura as the woman gestured to them to precede her. "I often think he looks at me in a very assessing way."

Maura and Lena chuckled as the hostess caught up with her aunt and led her into a sitting room.

The room was furnished primarily with Hepplewhite, the Adams fireplace the focal point. The rose and gold colors that predominated were both serene and pleasing to the eye.

Cyg sat down in a fireside settee across from Maura and Lena who occupied matching rose velvet side chairs.

The tray in front of them held a leaded crystal decanter and a bowl of dried banana slices.

"My nephew isn't here yet. He went down to the stables, but he promised he would be back for the lunch." Maura smiled sweetly. "I wouldn't dare offer him sherry . . . even dry, but I do hope you will join me in a glass."

"It's too early in the day for spirits." Lena Dilson glared at the leaded crystal decanter. "But, I'll make an exception. I'll pour." Lena had noticed just as Cyg had that Mrs. Tiebold had to edge the decanter closer to her so that she might grasp it with both hands. "Here, Cyg, you take one, too. Won't hurt you this once."

Cyg held the delicate crystal in her hand, turning it slowly so that the sunlight coming in the window made a rainbow in the amber liquid.

"I didn't know you drank anything this early in the day. In fact I was sure you stayed away from booze." The hard amusement in the masculine voice froze Cyg in place.

She couldn't have looked up had her life been the forfeit. The words of the others milled around her like wheeling gulls. She heard the noise, but didn't understand the message. Sounds bounced off her head. He was here in this room! He wasn't surprised to see her! She recognized Aunt Lena's laugh and murmur, but didn't know what she said. Maura said something, but what? Darius couldn't be here, Darius couldn't be here, Darius couldn't be here. The words ricocheted around her brain.

"Cyg. Cyg?" Aunt Lena demanded her attention.

"Yes." Cyg looked up, up, up into emerald eyes, gold specks raying out from the pupil. Darius was here. "How do you do?" She muttered, letting her gaze slide away from his face, her eyes fixing on a spray of white pinks in a green porcelain vase. She studied each curve and indentation in the intricately worked vase.

"This is my nephew, Darius Chadwick, Cyg." Maura pulled Cyg's eyes back to her with the words, her impish smile innocent. "I know you thought him to be younger, a teenager perhaps."

"Yes, I did," Cyg managed to say through woolly lips.

". . . I wanted to surprise you." Maura chuckled, lifting her wineglass to her lips and sipping.

"You did that," Cyg agreed, lifting her glass to her mouth and pouring the entire contents down her throat, then holding the glass out to her frowning aunt to be refilled.

Darius removed the glass from Cyg's hand, bringing the puzzled glances of the older women to his face. He continued to watch Cyg. "I don't think you want any more of this."

"Do too," Cyg muttered, staring at the cut-glass decanter and making up her mind to become a wino.

Darius lifted Cyg from the settee with one hand gripping her upper arm. "Aunt Maura, I'll bet Penny is about ready to serve that delicious gazpacho now."

"I said that I'd ring." His aunt blinked up at him.

Darius smiled at her, reached down, and pressed the button at the side of his aunt's chair. "There, I've done it for you. I'll show Miss Melton into the dining room."

"That's nice, dear," Maura said faintly.

Cyg didn't look at her aunt as she felt herself lifted from the room. "Put me down."

"I'm not carrying you." Darius's voice was just like the calm before a hurricane.

"You're dragging me," Cyg muttered, trying to pry her arm out of his hold.

"There you are. Free." Darius thrust her into a chair, none too gently.

"Listen you . . ." Cyg began before she saw his warning look.

Aunt Lena walked into the dining room at Maura Tiebold's side. "Cyg, what's the matter with you?"

"Nothing," Cyg mumbled, trying to keep a smile on her face.

"Don't tell me nothing. I know you too well." Lena stood in back of her chair, not allowing Darius to seat her as he had seated his aunt. She gave Darius her no nonsense look. "Do you know my niece?"

"Yes." He smiled at her, seating her then. "Ah, the salad looks good. Greens from Penny's garden, Aunt Maura?"

"Yes, dear. Some of the vegetables came from a man called Silvers who works at the Gideon, where you're staying." Maura was more easily diverted than was Lena.

"How long have you known my niece?" Lena pursued.

"Forever."

"Not long," Cyg croaked at the same time Darius spoke. When the three of them looked at her, she reached for her water glass, and drained it.

"Are you thirsty dear?" Maura asked.

Cyg nodded several times as she looked from Maura's glass to Lena's.

"Have some salad." Darius took the large bowl and began to ladle greens into Cyg's already full salad plate.

"No." Cyg could feel her lower jaw pushing out. She reached out to cover her plate with her hand, just as Darius tipped some onion slices toward her dish. She looked at the back of her hand now covered with bits of green pepper and escarole. "Hun." She glowered at Darius.

"I don't think she wanted quite so much salad dear." Maura had a hunted look to her as her gaze slid from her nephew to Cyg.

"Cygnet. Behave," Darius growled, removing the vegetables from Cyg's hand and putting them on an empty side plate.

"How do you know her name is Cygnet? Did you know her at school?" Lena Dilson wore her bulldog look, so Cyg didn't try to say anything.

"Not at school, Mrs. Dilson." Darius smiled at the older woman before taking a forkful of salad. He chewed slowly. "I'm several years older than Cygnet."

Lena pounced. "How old are you?"

"Darius will be thirty-seven in two weeks, won't you, dear?" Maura had a faraway smile. "He has always spent his birthdays with me, here in Saratoga, haven't you, dear?" She frowned for a moment. "Of course not the year you went on that climbing trip to Tibet, or the year you were at Oxford."

"That makes you almost ten years older than Cyg," Lena calculated.

Darius's brows, one shade deeper than his chestnut hair, rose. "Really? I thought you were younger than that . . . perhaps twenty-three."

"Bull," Cyg muttered, then reddened when Maura leaned toward her.

"Pardon, dear?" The older woman smiled at Cyg.

"Tell her Cygnet . . . Tell her what you said," Darius encouraged.

"I said . . . I'm full," Cyg lied, wanting to upend the gazpacho on his head.

"But my dear Cyg, you should eat more. You're so slender," Maura said.

"Skinny," Darius interjected.

"Am not," Cyg shot back, her hand clenching on her butter knife.

"Certainly you are not skinny, my dear." Maura looked at her nephew reproachfully. "Darius, what has gotten into you today?"

"Summer madness," he assured his aunt, bending over his cold soup once more.

Lena ate, darting sharp glances from her niece to Darius.

Cyg couldn't look her aunt in the eye.

After what seemed an interminable time to Cyg the lunch was over. She took hold of her aunt's arm as they were leaving the table. "I think I'll make my excuses and leave." Her smile felt wobbly.

"He's the man, isn't he?" Lena asked.

"Yes."

"Better to face him. I'll help you all I can."

Cyg gulped. "I love you Aunt Lena." She kissed her aunt, then followed her back into the sitting room. She went forward to speak to Mrs. Tiebold, but Darius got in the way.

He took a tight grip on her arm, his fingers squeezing when she tried to free herself. "I'm going to show Cygnet your formal garden, Aunt Maura, then I'll drive her home."

"No need to do that." Cyg's smile felt stretched. She couldn't free her arm, so she carefully lifted her foot. Keeping Darius as a shield in front of his aunt, she kicked him hard in the leg. When he flinched, she felt gleeful.

"Say good-bye nicely, Cygnet."

"Good by nicely," Cyg mumbled, then stepped

forward to take Mrs. Tiebold's hand and tell her how much she had enjoyed lunch. "Thank you for asking me."

"Oh, you're welcome, child. I've told Darius how helpful you've been to me and how I've wanted to have you at the house." She looked up at Darius and Cyg standing close together in front of her. "Isn't it amazing that you know each other?"

"Amazing." Cyg rolled her eyes at her aunt.

Aunt Lena walked over to them with purposeful strides. "Now see here . . ."

"I'll take the greatest care of her, no need to worry," Darius said.

Lena stared at him a long while, then nodded once and stepped back.

"Aunt Lena . . ." Cyg gasped.

"Go along, Cyg." Lena turned back to her hostess. "Tell me . . ."

She and Darius were out into the front hall before Cyg could say any more to her aunt. "Damn you, Darius, will you let go? My arm is getting numb."

"Then stop fighting me," he ordered, not releasing her, but loosening his grip.

Instead of taking her out the front door, he took her through the kitchen area of the house, exchanging a few quips with Penny before going out a back door, Cyg in tow.

"I don't want to go to the garden with you," Cyg hissed as soon as they were outside.

"All right." Darius was most amenable. He shepherded her toward a barn-like garage and pressed the button high on the door.

"If I had seen your car, I wouldn't have entered the house." Cyg spoke between her teeth.

"I know that. Did you have braces when you were younger?"

"Huh?" Cyg was off balance. "Yes, I did, not that it's any of your bus—"

"I thought so. You shouldn't grind your teeth

together like that after all the money your parents spent on your teeth." He pushed a shocked Cyg into the passenger seat, closed the door, and was around and in the driver's seat before she stopped sputtering.

"It may interest you to know . . ." She was so angry she was out of breath. ". . . that I never had any problems grinding my teeth until today."

"Good. Then you won't make a habit of it." Darius maneuvered the car out of the barn and around the house to the street.

"I'll have you arrested for harassment." Cyg made a conscious effort not to grind her teeth. "There's a law against coercing people."

"For visiting my aunt?" Darius asked, checking the traffic, then pulling out into the main street.

"You followed me," she accused, inhaling deeply. "You've been sneaking around Saratoga."

"I visit my aunt every year at this time," Darius said.

"Balderdash and twaddle," she shouted, her voice echoing around the air-conditioned car. "I'm not for sale."

"I love the way you curse, naughty lady." Darius chuckled.

Stung by the description he used, she lashed out. "I won't be your 'companion' or 'friend' or whatever you call it. I won't be your bloody mistress," she yelled, finding it hard to salivate.

"Wait until you're damn well asked," Darius roared back, swerving around the car in front of him, making the driver shake his head. "And why the hell are you talking that funny way?"

Cyg hauled in a deep breath. "How dare you mock the way I speak you Oxfordian halfwit? I wasn't shuffled around from school to school because I had a kindergarten mentality." Cyg lifted her chin. "Why don't you stick to party girls?"

"Are you intimating that I am a witless fool?"

His voice had dropped a decibel. "And I think you were partying when I met you."

"I think the term witless fool is redundant, but, if you feel the description fits . . ." Cyg lifted her hands palms upward, fighting the hurt at his words.

"Damn you, woman, I don't take slurs from anyone." Darius jerked the wheel of the car and it whipped alarmingly around the curve in the road.

"When the police pick you up for reckless driving, I shall be a witness against you."

"How civic-minded of you," Darius spat at her.

"Turn here. There's Birch Street." Cyg spaced her words as though she were instructing a slow learner.

"Thank you." Darius turned into the short driveway so fast that Cyg was sure he would plow right into the ancient garage that was already listing a few degrees to the left.

As she turned to get out of the car, he gripped her arm again. "Would you stop doing that?" She glowered at him. "You're making marks on me."

"I don't want to do that . . . not on my property." He lifted her arm to his mouth.

She yanked it free. "I'm no one's property."

"You're mine, and don't forget it. Now that I've found you, I'm keeping my eye on you . . . until you come to your senses."

"Found me? Until I come to my senses?" She choked on her anger. "Just what do you think—"

Darius interrupted her by reaching across her and pushing the door open. "Out. I'm in a hurry."

Cyg alighted from the car, then turned to look at him, ready for battle.

Darius reversed out of the driveway like a cyclone in retreat.

"You don't scare me," Cyg shouted at the disappearing vehicle through her cupped hands.

When she turned to go in the house, Mr. Brownell, Aunt Lena's neighbor, was leaning on his fence.

"Nice car your boyfriend's got."

"That madman is *not* my boyfriend." Cyg glared in the direction Darius had gone.

"Looked like it." Mr. Brownell picked up his hoe and went back to weeding his garden.

Cyg opened her mouth to argue with Mr. Brownell, then brought her teeth together with a snap, almost running into the house.

The next evening Steve came over. Cyg looked at him blankly.

"Did you forget we were going for a bike ride?" Steve asked.

Cyg pressed her hand against her forehead. Damn that Darius Chadwick! He was really getting to her. "Yes, I did forget. It'll only take me a minute to change into jeans and sneakers." Cyg whirled into the house, not wanting Steve to change his mind. She needed the exercise of riding her bike. It would help to rid her of those constant thoughts of Darius.

Aunt Lena stood in the driveway waving to Cyg and Steve, telling them to be sure and use their lights once it was dark.

Cyg could feel Steve's frequent glances, recognizing his puzzlement without even looking at him. There was no way she could explain Darius to Steve, even if she wanted to—and she didn't want to.

"Hey, lady, are we training for the cross-country run, or what?" Steve panted as they pedaled up another hill.

Cyg pulled her bike to one side of the road at the top, puffing but feeling exhilarated. "I was feeling pretty woolly today. I needed the exercise."

"Oh, I thought you were trying to wear me out so that I didn't try to . . . seduce you tonight," Steve panted, giving her his best out-of-breath leer.

"My Aunt Lena told me I'd be able to fight off mashers if I kept working out." Cyg waggled her index finger at him as she leaned on her handlebars.

"Me? A masher?" Steve looked pleased. "Wait until I tell my grandmother. A success at last."

"You fool." Cyg laughed, feeling more relaxed. She inhaled the soft night air deeply, its balmy cleanness soothing her. "Saratoga is a lovely place."

"I think you're staring to repeat yourself. That's a sign of senility."

Cyg grabbed at his bike, trying to shake him off it. They were roughhousing and laughing when the Ferrari went by, screeched to a stop, reversed with a roar, then sped off again sending loose stones into the air.

"What a car! Did you see that Cyg?" Steve whistled, not looking at her.

"I saw it." She swallowed.

"He must have thought he knew us," Steve said, mounting his bike and following Cyg down the winding country road, his off-key singing of a Beatles' tune having an echo chamber sound in the stillness of twilight. Purple night chased the orange shadows of day as they headed toward the center of town and the soda fountain they were in the habit of frequenting.

Cyg felt the hair lifting on her arms as she took a long pull at her chocolate soda. She knew before she looked up that Darius was there. Even from the distance of the soda fountain back to the booth where she was sitting with Steve, Cyg could smell the sulfur. Darius was in a rage. She felt like a butterfly pinned to a board, unable to move, legs not obeying her order to run, disappear. Though Darius had never shown temper to her while they were together at Phil Tabor's house, she could remember his arbitrary treatment of persons or things that displeased him. Anger seemed to smoke out of him, fill the air, filter down to her booth, and dry up her taste buds, corroding her love for chocolate.

"Soda not good tonight?" Steve asked, spooning some of his ice cream from the bottom of his glass into his mouth.

"Ah . . . sometimes, when I'm getting a cold, things don't taste the same," Cyg croaked, telling herself that Darius was civilized and he wouldn't dare tear the place down. "I think we should go."

"Yeah." Steve gave her his full attention as he wiped his mouth. "Your voice does sound funny." He reached down to her side of the booth and retrieved the sweater she was about to leave behind. "Maybe you should put this on and not just tie it round your neck."

"No . . . no. Don't need it. Warm out." Cyg hurried Steve past Darius, looking away from him.

"Good evening, Cygnet."

"Evening." Cyg pushed at Steve when he would have paused, rushing him when he paid the tab, urging him out the door.

"Who was that?" Steve craned his neck trying to see over Cyg's shoulder as she pushed him from behind.

"Nobody."

"Nobody?" Steve dug in his heels forcing her to stop pushing him toward the bikes. "Well, if he's nob . . . Wow!" Steve's attention refocused on the Ferrari parked at the curb. "There's the silver bullet again." He frowned at Cyg. "Stop looking glassy-eyed. You remember the car that screeched to a stop on Jones Road?"

"Yes."

"This is the same one." Steve leaned over her. "Your voice is getting more hoarse every minute."

Cyg blinked up at him for a long moment. "Yes . . . yes, it is getting worse. Let's go. Can't be sick. Gotta job." Cyg was about to unlock her bike when Steve took her arm.

"Wait a minute. I don't get that many chances

to look at these babies. C'mon. Let's check it out." Steve urged her toward the gleaming low-slung vehicle.

She approached it with all the enthusiasm of climbing into bed with a cobra. "Seen enough. Let's go."

"Right," Steve mumbled as he pressed his face against the glass on the driver's side, his one hand acting as a visor as he stared into the interior of the car. "What a beauty," he crowed.

"Would you like to take it for a spin?"

Cyg had braced herself for his approach but she jumped just the same when Darius spoke. She glared at him. "Sneak."

"I beg your pardon?" His face looked like an ice sculpture.

"Nothing," she muttered, glancing away from him and back to Steve. "Time to go, Steve," she hissed.

"Did you really say 'would you like to take a spin'?" Steve ignored Cyg and walked right up to Darius.

"Yes. Go ahead. I'll stay here with your friend." Darius's mellow voice sounded doomlike to Cyg.

"I'll go with Steve. Steve? I'll go with you. Right?"

"Huh? Oh, sure." Steve walked around the front of the car, the keys cradled in his hands, unlocked the door, and slid into the driver's seat. He didn't unlock Cyg's door until she banged on the window.

As she started to slide into the seat, Darius swept her up into his arms and sat with her in the front seat. "Release me," she grated.

"Remember your orthodontia." He turned his head to look at Steve who only seemed minimally surprised to see Cyg on Darius's lap. "Yes, that's how to start it. Relax." Darius instructed Steve as the younger man jerked the car a bit in first gear. Darius's arms tightened on Cyg as Steve concentrated on his driving.

When Cyg felt his fingers gently kneading her buttocks, she stiffened. "Deviate," she cursed him.

"Not so," he whispered back.

"Let me go . . . you . . . you molester."

"Never. You're mine." Darius grunted when she pinched his neck. "And don't label me with dirty words."

"You *are* a dirty word." Cyg couldn't resist nipping his cheek.

"Ouch," Darius's hand squeezed her backside.

"Oh, sorry," Steve said, a guilty tinge to his voice. "Did I take that curve too fast?"

"You have to watch the fast movers. They take off on you," Darius drawled, looking at Cyg.

"Right," Steve answered. "This is the greatest machine I ever drove," he said as he pulled over to the curb in front of the soda fountain. He turned with a smile to look at Darius, then frowned as though he noticed for the first time that Cyg was on Darius's lap.

Before he could say anything, Darius was out of his car with Cyg in his arms. He deposited her on the sidewalk, none too gently, his hand going at once to his right cheek.

Steve came around the car, the keys held out in front of him. "That was great. Thanks. My name's Steve . . . Hey, you have quite a mark on your cheek. What happened?"

Darius took his keys, walked around the car, and looked over the hood from Steve to Cyg and back again. "I tangled with a cat. I intend to be more careful next time."

The car roared away like an angry silver cheetah.

Six

The next morning when she woke, Darius's face was there in the camera image of her mind. Her cold shower didn't dispel him; the image only sharpened.

"Damn you, go away," Cyg muttered as she clattered down the narrow stairway to the kitchen.

She burned her mouth on the coffee and spilled a drop of orange juice on her lemon-colored cotton jeans. Then she tripped on her untied sneaker lace and spilled shredded wheat on the linoleum. By the time she cleaned up her spills and sponged the mark out of her jeans, much of her time was limping away. She noticed her aunt's note by accident; it told her that Mr. Brownell was away for a few days and asked if she would mind exercising Waldo, his basset hound.

"Lord, I'll be late," Cyg mumbled as she climbed over the fence into Mr. Brownell's yard. "Stop that barking, Waldo, I'm your exercise girl." She glared at the low slung black-and-tan creature who both barked and wagged his tail at the same time. "Stop that noise. You don't sound like a dog, you soung like a stopped-up sink."

Waldo's idea of exercise was to wander through fields and avoid pavement of any kind. Despite his closeness to the ground, Waldo had a good deal of strength and succeeded in pulling Cyg where he wanted her to go. When he tangled her around a neighbor's flagpole, making the lady of the house stare through her venetian blinds, Cyg called it quits.

Straining and pulling and getting red-faced, Cyg was at last able to get Waldo into his own yard and lock the gate. Her hands had red marks from pulling on the leather leash, she was sure her blood pressure had gone through the roof, and she needed another shower. She leaned against the fence, panting, looking down at the placid, soulful animal, who stared back at her, his tail wagging in slow cadence. "You are . . . without a doubt . . . the most stubborn dog . . . I have ever known. And now I don't have time . . . for a shower." She gnashed her teeth, then clambered over the wooden fence again, running first to get her knapsack, then to get her bike.

She was later than usual and the traffic was heavier. When the third driver honked at her as he raced by her, she shook her fist in the air, making her front wheel wobble.

When another car pulled alongside, idling next to her as she panted and pedaled red-faced up an incline, she was ready to commit murder.

"Want a lift?"

Darius! Cyg looked sideways for just a moment. Her bike hit some soft gravel and shook. She fought to keep from tumbling from the seat. "Hit and run!" Cyg yelled at him, wishing she had a rock to throw through the windshield of the Ferrari.

"Calm down, Cygnet. Your face is tomato red." Darius spoke easily through the lowered window on the passenger side of the car.

"Don't you laugh at me, you . . . you highway man." Cyg choked, trying to pedal faster.

"Will you be careful, for heaven's sake?" Darius

called out to her as she skidded to a stop at the signal light that would carry her across the highway and into the park road.

"Go away," Cyg hissed, steadying her bike and watching the light, praying it would change fast.

"Wait a minute . . ." Darius opened the door on the driver's side of the car.

The light changed. Cyg hopped on her bike and shot across the four lanes of traffic into the park road. She didn't turn her head when she heard horns blowing. She almost cackled with delight as she pictured Darius arguing with the drivers of the autos behind him as he held up traffic. She wheeled down the path toward the Roosevelt Baths, stopped, then chained her bike to the rack. She felt terribly grimy and sweaty.

Entering the building, she went around to the reception area to explain to Claudia why she was late in case Wentworth was looking for her.

"Do you have an appointment? You can't have a . . ." Claudia stared up at Cyg.

"Claudia, it's me," Cyg grated out.

"I don't care if you're the Queen of England, you can't have a massage without an appointment."

Cyg held her breath, her fingers itching to grip Claudia's throat, then stalked to the employees' locker room, taking the time to shower before she donned the nurselike white dress that was her uniform. She was still buttoning the garment when she went to find her aunt.

"Ah, there you are, Cyg. Did Waldo give you any trouble?" Her aunt had a pile of towels in her arms which Cyg took from her.

"No." Cyg read her patrons' names from the list Aunt Lena held in front of her.

"Ah." Her aunt nodded. "Waldo pulled you through the fields, did he?" Her aunt smiled when Cyg glared at her. "I should have warned you. Waldo has a mind of his own."

"Surprise, surprise." Cyg turned her back on

her aunt's laughter and stalked to her first cubicle. She turned on the faucets with vicious twists of her hands. Cyg visualized Darius as the faucets. As the hot effervescent water streamed into the over-sized tubs, frothing and curling, Cyg didn't really see it. She saw instead Darius's face. "Damn the man, I will not spend my life looking at him wherever I go. I'll blot him out of my mind if I have to pour ink in my ear."

"Eh? Ink in your ear?" Marianne almost lifted her gaze to eye level, she was that interested. "Is that good for wax?" The older woman shuffled forward a centimeter at a time.

"I was talking to myself," Cyg muttered.

Marianne nodded sagely. "Got money in the bank. I knew a banker once. Ran off with all the money in his bank." Marianne nodded again. "Liked him. He was honest."

"He was a thief," Cyg pointed out.

"Yep . . . but he never pretended to be anything else. And all bankers are thieves." Marianne began humming as she shuffled out of the cubicle after depositing the bottle of body lotion Cyg would need.

"What worries me . . ." Cyg lifted the lotion bottle and spoke to it, ". . . is that she's starting to make sense. I had better book a room in the local happy farm." Cyg slammed down the container of emollient and left the room to get her first patron of the day.

When she heard the loud voices arguing, she paused before entering the reception area. She looked through the glass partition and almost fainted. Darius was arguing with Claudia! Where was Wentworth? Had he gone to one of those meetings that he never seemed to stop attending? Cyg wondered as she cowered behind the door and tried to hear what Darius was saying . . . no, shouting. Darius was angry!

"What in the name of heaven is going on?" Aunt

Lena came out of one of the massage rooms, her sleeves rolled up, arms akimbo.

"Shhhh." Cyg gestured to her. "Darius is arguing with Claudia."

"I will not shush." Aunt Lena hauled in a deep breath, pushed each sleeve farther up her arm, and jutted out her chin. "No one makes a fuss in the Roosevelt Baths," she pronounced in solemn tones, her voice down a decibel.

Marianne shuffled out of a room, taking long seconds to look from Cyg to Lena to the reception area door. "Communists?" Her adenoids were more defined, as she tried to breathe.

"Hooligan." Aunt Lena breathed, ready to smite the Philistine.

Cyg stepped in front of her aunt as Lena moved toward the swinging doors leading to the reception area. "If we ignore him, he'll go away." Cyg crossed her fingers behind her back.

"He doesn't sound as though he'll go away." Lena Dilson looked grim.

"Is he a sex maniac?" Marianne stared through the wired safety glass, blinking myopically.

"You sound hopeful," Cyg said waspishly.

"Cyg, stop it." Her aunt frowned at her, then glowered at the other woman. "Of course he isn't a sex maniac. What made you think that?"

"Well, "Marianne wheezed, "I'm no expert on sex maniacs, but I think they're usually tall." She pointed to the gesturing Darius whose mouth was snapping like a bear trap. "He's tall."

"Might I remind you that Abraham Lincoln was tall," Aunt Lena said curtly.

"Oh? Was he a sex maniac?" Marianne asked oblivious to the fact that Lena was sputtering. She turned and shuffled back into her cubicle, mumbling, "Never did like a man with a beard."

Cyg gulped a shaky laugh.

Aunt Lena shook her head. "That woman flummoxes me." She stopped speaking and cocked her head at the sound of squealing wheels and grinding gears. "I think our noisy intruder has taken a powder as they say. Let's get back to work Cyg." Aunt Lena disappeared into her cubbyhole, saying, "Now, Mrs. Lehrman, we're done, aren't we?"

Cyg sagged against the wall, feeling as though her veins had clogged and her arteries had done a U turn. While she leaned against the wall, she plotted Darius's murder. It wasn't bad enough that he had embarrassed her in front of her aunt and Mrs. Tiebold, now he was making scenes at the baths.

She hurried back to her cubicle, apologizing for being away so long. "Wrong? No, nothing was wrong, Mrs. Dene. There was a nut at the front desk but he's been removed."

Darius was on her mind all day. Mrs. Kline complained when Cyg massaged her leg too hard. "I'm sorry, I was thinking of . . . er . . . my mind was wandering."

Cyg's daydreams of throwing him into Lake George with a boulder tied to his neck, backing Mr. Brownell's riding lawn mower over him three or four times had her smiling through her lunch hour.

"No way am I hooking myself up with a man who thinks I'm a call girl," Cyg gritted to herself as she pedaled to her afternoon job at the Gideon. "I made the mistake of getting involved with Darius once, but I'm smarter now. I have no feeling for the man except a strong desire to see him flung off the roof of the Gideon." She smothered the voice inside her that kept jeering "Oh, yeah? Oh, yeah?" No way would she hook up with a man who wanted a part-time pillow friend. She knew enough girls in New York who had that deal. You don't see them on the holidays . . . that's set aside for family. The mistress is just plain set aside. Not for her, the lonely Christmas Eves while honey bun is off visiting the wife. Wife! Darius said he was divorced. He lied! Cyg slammed her bike into the rack and locked it, cursing Darius, his wife, his family, and all his friends, all the way back to his kindergarten teacher.

She walked into the kitchen and glared around her.

"Are you upset, Cyg?" Silvers said, gesturing for her to take a chair, then bringing a huge spinach salad to place in front of her.

"No." She forked a plate-sized spinach leaf into her mouth. She chewed three times on one side of her mouth, three on the other. "I have just decided not to murder a snake. I'll let someone else kill him."

Silvers poured her a glass of milk. "Good idea . . . oh, not to kill snakes at all, they are good for keeping the mice out of the garden, but I am glad that *you* don't wish to kill it."

"This snake is six-foot-three and weighs about one hundred and ninety pounds." Cyg speared a slice of mushroom and popped it into her mouth.

"A python got loose from the zoo, you think?" Silvers looked worried.

"Huh?" Cyg dabbed her mouth with the cloth napkin. "Oh . . . Don't worry, Silvers. He won't be anywhere near your garden."

"Good. I wouldn't want him killing my toad."

"*He is a toad*," Cyg pronounced, rising to her feet and placing the napkin next to her plate.

"Oh? It's not a snake?" Silvers was bewildered.

Cyg kissed his forehead. "Don't worry. I'll buy a fine pest killer." She waved to the kitchen staff and pushed through the doors to the corridor that would take her to the front desk. She was hoping it would be Steve she was relieving so that she could ask him if he wanted to play tennis one day at the club. She had the feeling that Darius would be around the house and she didn't want to be there, if she could manage it.

She read the notes on the spindle and called the

rooms indicated in the message book. She sensed someone at the desk in front of her and looked up smiling. "*You.*"

"Yes, me," Darius replied. "I'm a guest in this place and I expect the kind of treatment a guest deserves." A muscle jumped in his jaw; his face looked like it had been chiseled on Mount Rushmore.

"Of course, sir. What can I do for you?" Cyg kept her voice flat.

"What time do you get off tonight?"

"That's none of your business," she snapped.

"I can ask the manager."

"Then ask him." She glared.

Darius leaned forward just a fraction, but all at once Cyg felt hemmed in, stifled.

"You're pushing me a little too hard, lady, and I don't like it."

"Then stuff it in your ear," Cyg said, closing her eyes for a moment as Darius loomed further over the desk.

"I'm warning you, Cygnet, I will not put up with this crap much longer. Just what the hell do you think you're doing? I've played your game long enough—"

"Pardon me, but isn't this where you register?"

Darius stepped back and a tiny lady in a seersucker suit smiled at Cyg.

"I'm Mrs. Vander Water." She lifted her pince-nez and set them on her nose, bending her head back to look at Darius. "It is you, isn't it? Darius William! I thought as much. But when I heard you shouting at this young lady, I didn't think it could be the nephew of my dear friend, Maura. What has happened to you, dear boy, that you would raise your voice?"

"Naturally bad mannered?" Cyg offered, pushing Mrs. Vander Water's key toward her.

"Oh, no, my dear, Darius William was always a polite boy. Of course he was a scamp, too . . ." Mrs.

Vander Water patted Darius on the forearm. ". . . but a polite boy just the same."

"He's changed." Cyg lifted her chin at the carved marble of Darius Chadwick's face.

"I shall escort you to your room, Lettie." He smiled down at the miniscule person, then looked back at Cyg. "Then I shall be back to wait until your shift is over."

Cyg sat against the back of the high stool, feeling the heat emanating from Darius.

When he returned to the lobby he had a briefcase which he opened like a desk. He didn't so much as glance at her for the rest of the evening. There were many quiet moments when they might have talked, but Darius continued to work, not bothering to look her way.

At quarter to eleven, Steve came on. "Hi. Anything doing?"

"Not much," Cyg replied, giving him a big smile. "Would you like to play tennis . . . say, Thursday?"

"Sure. Make it around noon. I have to come on at two that day."

Cyg let her eyes slide in Darius's direction. He was busy writing. "Why don't we make it eleven-thirty. I'm through at the baths at eleven."

"Fine." Steve shuffled through the messages.

"See you," Cyg whispered, glancing once more at the busy Darius, then backing out the door.

She heaved a sigh of relief as she finished in the locker room in record time and scampered out to get her bike.

She squinted at the bike rack, the bright-as-day night lights on the grounds illuminating the park-like area surrounding the hotel. "My bike is gone," Cyg spoke out loud. "Who would want to steal Old Nuts and Bolts?" she asked the night air.

"Your bike is in the trunk of my car." Darius leaned against a giant maple tree.

Cyg jumped, then snapped at him, "It wouldn't fit," wishing she could back his Ferrari over him.

"Stealing is still a crime in this part of the country."

"Now you're a lawyer . . . Delightful!" Darius took her arm above the elbow, propelling her a little in front of him to the row of cars lining the half-moon of the drive.

"Stop that. Don't you push me around, buster," Cyg sputtered, feeling herself thrust into the car.

"Then stop acting like a child. I told you that we were going to talk and I meant it." Darius started the car with a roar, angling away from the car in front of him before shooting around the drive and out the exit.

"I hope you get a ticket." Cyg spoke through her teeth. The words hardly had left her mouth when Darius flung the car down one of the tree-lined roads, then screeched to a stop on a grassy shoulder. "And don't try to intimidate me." Cyg coughed to clear the quaver from her voice.

"I am not trying to intimidate you," Darius barked. "I . . ."

"Then why are you shouting?" Cyg interrupted, feeling her temper begin to rise.

"I am not shouting," Darius yelled. "If you would stop—"

"Then I don't know what you call it, you Oxfordian lout," Cyg riposted, her voice raising a decibel.

"Listen to me." Darius grabbed her by the shoulders and turned her toward him.

"Ouch! Your damn gear box is digging into me." Cyg pushed against him.

"Sorry. I guess a car isn't the best place to do this." Darius let her lean back into her seat. "Would you come to my suite?"

"At the Gideon?" Cyg squawked. "Not bloody likely."

"Did you study in England, too?" Darius asked, interested.

"Stuff it, buster."

"Will you stop talking like a dock worker and listen to me for a minute?"

"Don't you try to label me, you . . . you fugitive from Ding Dong School," Cyg gasped, rage filling her with multicolored meteors.

"For God's sake woman, do you never listen?" Darius bellowed, lifting her out of her seat to lay her across his body. "I want to speak to you and I want you to listen to me. Is that clear?" His face was inches from hers.

Cyg was cross-eyed staring at him. "Your hands are caving in my rib cage," she panted. "I'll listen."

"Good." He set her back in her seat once more. The silence stretched between them.

When she saw him rubbing his hands together, she frowned. If it were anyone else she would say he was nervous. Darius was not the type to be nervous, she concluded, then turned back to stare out the windshield, determined not to say anything until he spoke.

"I am . . . I think . . . My aunt would expect us . . . Never mind. This is not the proper place." He took a deep breath. "My aunt tells me that the reason you were able to come for lunch was because Thursday was your short day."

"Right."

"Well, ah . . . I'll take you out on Thursday and—"

"I have a date." Cyg relished telling him that.

"What? You have a date? What the hell! Break it," he demanded.

"No."

Darius expelled the air from his nose.

"And don't snort at me," Cyg said waspishly.

"I'm not snorting," he roared back. "When are you free?"

"In a week and a half."

"Cygnet, I'm warning you. I won't put up with it. When do you get an evening off next? And I want the truth."

"I don't lie . . ." she shouted, then muttered ". . . unless I have to."

"It's a good thing you qualified that." Darius was grim. "Now tell me when you have a free evening."

"Tomorrow night." She looked out the side window as the car cruised down Birch Street.

"You're going to see me everywhere, Cygnet, and if you try to run out on me again, I'll wrap you in chains . . . and you can bet your bottom on that." He came around to her side of the car and opened the door.

"Macho is already a has-been word . . . and so are macho men." She tried to free her arm from his hands.

"I've tried being a nice guy with you. It didn't work." He turned her to face him, his sudden smile making her blink. "You look like a pugnacious pussycat."

"And I can scratch."

"Scratch away." Darius lifted her up until their eyes were level, his mouth taking hers in small tender bites. "Scratch, bite, kick, do your worst. It won't change the inevitable."

Before Cyg could ask him what the inevitable was, his mouth had fixed to hers like a homing device. His mouth persuaded, coaxed, teased, before passion took them both.

Cyg felt that even if Darius's arms released her, she wouldn't fall away from his body. She felt connected to him by forces of electricity. When his tongue teased hers, her pulse lost two whole beats. Her brain instructed her to push free of him, listing seventy logical reasons in as many milliseconds. Cyg clutched at him as though he were the only raft in a reenactment of the Great Flood. When he would have pulled back from her, she moaned, and dug her fingers into his neck.

"Cygnet, for God's sake . . ." Darius breathed, his mouth scouring down her cheek. "I'll be making love to you in your aunt's driveway." His voice held a husky note of amusement.

"Huh?" Cyg reeled back from him, glad his arms were steadying her. She blinked up at him. "Can't do that. Good night." She staggered, then forced herself to march toward her aunt's door. She didn't turn around when he chuckled and whispered, "Good night."

Cyg had the nightmare again that night. She was down on her knees begging Darius to love her and he was standing above her, laughing, a blond on each arm, telling them that this, and he pointed down at Cyg, was a call girl he used to know.

She woke at dawn, the usual time, her shaking hand wiping moisture from her cheeks. No, no, no, it wasn't worth it. She wasn't going to compromise all the future happiness in life there might be for her by taking a chance with Darius. If she stayed with him, became his mistress, sooner or later he would want out of the commitment, he would want to marry someone his family would like, he would want children . . .

Cyg sat bolt upright in bed. Who was the woman who would have Darius's children? God! She covered her face with her hands. She didn't want to know. She would make sure when Darius married that she would be out of the country . . . off the planet, maybe.

She hopped out of bed, racing for the shower, forcing Darius's picture from her mind with needles of cold water. She would have nothing more to do with the man. She would tell him tonight that she wanted him to leave her alone.

Pedaling to work sanded off some of the rough edges that the nightmare had given her. She inhaled deep breaths and waved to some of the drivers who passed her, and shook her fist at others.

When she heard a car pull up behind her, its engine a low growl, she knew who it was before Darius spoke.

"Tomorrow I'll be biking with you to work. I don't like the idea of you being alone." His low tones came to her from the window.

"I'm all right." She didn't look his way.

"Nevertheless, I'll be biking with you tomorrow. Shall I pick you up after work this afternoon?"

"No." She lowered her voice. "No." She steadied the bike. "Pick me up at seven."

"Six-thirty," Darius amended. "By the way, did I tell you that you have the roundest, cutest bottom I have ever seen. I don't like it that other motorists are seeing what I'm seeing." A horn blared behind Darius.

"You're holding up traffic," Cyg bleated, wishing he would go away, hating her body because her pulse rate had increased and her heart was thumping, and not from pedaling the bike.

Darius followed her in his car right to the baths, then waved to her and roared away.

That day Maura Tiebold was one of her patrons. Cyg found it hard to converse with the gentle woman.

"My dear, I was delighted when Darius told me that you and he were very close." Maura's light laughter went over Cyg's skin like the rasping of a nail on a blackboard. "Isn't it amusing that we talked about my nephew for so long and yet neither of us made the connection?"

"Amusing," Cyg agreed, feeling her smile crack across her face.

"Darius has told me that you are very special to him, Cygnet, dear." The older woman continued to chatter while Cyg placed the cloth under her chin while she soaked in the hot bath.

"That was . . . before." Cyg managed to say, then fled the room before the puzzled Maura could quiz her more.

When she saw how busy her aunt was for the rest of the morning and the long list of patrons for the afternoon, she approached Lena. "I could work this evening, if you like . . ."

Lena frowned at her. "Nonsense. The work will be handled as usual. Quitting time is five. Besides, you have a date."

"I'll break it."

"No need." Aunt Lena rolled up her sleeves before entering a room.

Cyg even called the Gideon to see if they would want her to work that evening. They didn't need her.

When she pedaled home from work, she ran every excuse to break the date around in her head. She was sure Darius would shoot holes in every one.

She dawdled. She flipped through the few summer dresses she had, settling at last on a little nothing dress that was three years old, another holdover from the stocking account days when she had had enough money to indulge in a few good dresses. It was black silk that had the look of cotton eyelet and was cut straight across the top of the breasts, falling in pleats from a belted waist. When she moved, the material floated outward in a bell shape. Under it she wore a black half-slip and black bikini pants . . . but no bra. She twisted her long curling hair into a blond rope that she coiled on the top of her head. Two long curls hung down her left cheek. With the outfit she wore jet earrings that had belonged to her great grandmother and an oblong jet ring on the third finger of her right hand. Her heels were high, black leather slides, her stockings the sheerest shadowy black.

When she finished dressing, Cyg went downstairs, hearing Aunt Lena moving around the kitchen.

Lena Dilson studied her niece for a long moment. "I used to think your mother was one of the prettiest gals I ever knew . . . and she was. But you, my child, are beautiful."

"Aunt Lena," Cyg choked, moving forward to hug the woman who had never spoken about love too much, but had always been there.

They stood there, looking at one another.

"I want you to be happy Cyg." Aunt Lena patted her shoulder just as the doorbell rang at the front of the house.

Cyg could see Darius on the other side of the screen door as she went down the hall. "Come in."

"Are you ready?" Darius held the screen door wide.

"Come in, Aunt Lena is here." Cyg cleared her throat, her gaze sliding away from him as his eyes went over her.

"You're beautiful." Darius's voice was husky.

"That's what I said." Lena came down the short hall from the kitchen.

"I think we agree on many things, Mrs. Dilson." Darius chuckled, making Cyg frown and look from her aunt to Darius.

"Yes, I think so, too," Lena said, her face bland as she reached up to kiss Cyg on the cheek. "Good night."

Cyg let Darius hand her into the car, but the moment he got behind the wheel, she turned to him. "What did you mean when you said that to my aunt? About agreeing with her?"

"Hmmmm? Oh . . . I'll tell you later." He maneuvered his car down the narrow street. "Like music?" His hand hovered over the tape deck.

"Yes." Cyg felt unsettled and tried to relax in the air-conditioned comfort of the car.

"I thought we would stop at the racetrack first. I want to take a look at one of my horses." Darius weaved through the traffic of downtown Saratoga.

"You have horses here?" Cyg spoke in a faint voice. "Running? At Saratoga?"

"Yes. Darby's Man and Excalibur. Know them?"

"Yes . . . no." Cyg tried to clear the squeak from

her voice. "I was at the stables a week ago. I saw their names."

"Who was with you?" Darius barked.

"Don't grill me!" Cyg snapped back. "I'm not a prisoner and you're not my keeper."

"No? We'll see about that," Darius snapped.

Cyg had the feeling that a tiger shark's voice would sound pretty much the same . . . if it could speak. She shivered. "Don't threaten me," she muttered, flicking her eyes over him and away again.

"I am not threatening you . . . just spelling it out. For a so-called intelligent woman, you can be damned obtuse."

"Don't you call me stupid," Cyg flared, feeling her blood race.

"I did not call you stupid." Darius spoke in measured tones, swinging into the parking lot of the racetrack and maneuvering the car close to the stables. He stopped so quickly that Cyg was thrown against her seat belt. "Very soon you'll have to start understanding what I mean, Cygnet. I've been damned patient."

"Of all the blustering, pompous . . ." Cyg hauled in deep breaths.

"And stop interrupting everything that I say." He came around the front of the car to open Cyg's door, but she was out before he reached it, standing there facing him, her clenched fists on her hips.

"Listen, buster, you . . ."

He took her arms, pushed them behind her back, and planted a quick hard kiss on her mouth. "The name's Darius."

". . . are not my boss," Cyg wheezed, trying to get air into her lungs and force her body to not collapse against him.

Darius placed a hard arm across her shoulders and guided her through to the exercise area in front of the stables. He waved to a short bandy legged man, who had a flattened cigarette hanging from the side of his mouth. "Hello, Bobby. How's it going?"

"Well enough." The little man turned his close-set eyes on Cyg. "The little woman?" he grunted.

Darius laughed. "Not yet."

Cyg pushed free of Darius's arm. "What do you mean 'not yet'?" She felt a war cry bubble inside her.

"Tall . . . but skinny." The man called Bobby ran an assessing eye over her. "Good legs, a money filly, to be sure. Fatten her up and she'll go the distance." Bobby mumbled around the cigarette that had almost burned to his lip.

Cyg moved toward the shorter man, all her anger toward Darius boiling to the surface.

Darius caught her around the waist, shackling her wriggling body to his side with no effort. "We came to see The Man and Excalibur."

"They'll run," the taciturn Bobby ventured, moving away from them and walking back into the darkened stables.

Cyg tried to free herself from Darius's hold. She glared up at him, ready to do battle.

"Look behind you, Cygnet," Darius said in a low tone, looking over her head.

She turned around to stare into the velvet eyes of a bay-colored thoroughbred. His eyes were set wide apart showing his Arabian strain. He sidled, throwing up his head and snorting at the lowly humans facing him. "Oh, you beauty!" Cyg crooned, forgetting all about Darius and the crusty Bobby. She stepped closer. The horse shook his head.

"Ain't no meanness in Darby's Man," Bobby offered. "But he likes to get to know you before he calls you chum." The laconic trainer touched the animal on the nose. Darby immediately nickered.

"Of course," Cyg said with assurance. "He's too bright to mix with strangers." She clasped her hands in front of her and watched Darby as he watched her.

"She'll do," Bobby said to Darius.

"Yes," Darius answered back.

Cyg was thrilled to see Excalibur then, too, but she didn't feel the same affinity she had experienced with Darby's Man.

When it was time to leave, she shook Bobby's hand and thanked him for letting her see the horses.

"Come again." Bobby waved and went back to the stable.

She didn't try to pull away when Darius twined his fingers with hers on the way back to the car. "Thank you. I've visited the stable before, but I never get tired of it."

Darius's fingers tightened on hers. "Do you know other owners?"

"No. I used to run errands for friends of my uncle's who were workers here." She looked up at him and smiled. "This is the first time I've met anyone who actually owned horses. I enjoyed seeing them."

"Especially Darby's Man." Darius chuckled.

Cyg let him hand her into the car, nodding. "That was fun."

"Now we'll eat. I hope you're as hungry as I am, but not so hungry you'll faint. We're driving to a French restaurant called Chez Elise just outside Glens Falls."

"Oh?" Cyg tried not to picture other women he had taken there. "Have you been there often?"

"Yes."

"Sounds great," she mumbled, rubbing her smudged hands together. "I hope they have a washroom. My hands are dirty."

"Oh, I think they do." Darius chuckled.

She glared at his profile, etched in the light of the dying sun, wishing he was ugly and scarred, then moaning inside because she knew that it wouldn't matter what he looked like; she would not be able to help loving him. Maybe if he were only three feet tall she would grow to dislike him, she mused; after all how comfortable could it be to keep bending from the waist to communicate with someone. Damn the man, I'd love him if I had to get down on my knees to talk to him, she told herself angrily.

Chez Elise was small, intimate, yet homey.

Cyg was incensed to be yet again one-upped when Darius responded in fluent French to the greeting of the *maîtresse d'*. "Don't tell me that you also attended school in France!" she said between clenched teeth.

"Wrong!" Darius whispered as they followed the older woman. "I worked summers on a fishing boat out of the Marseilles harbor, and sometimes spent Christmas in Paris with a friend."

The *maîtresse d'* showed them to a secluded corner. The round table was covered with lavender and pink linen; the fragrance from an orchid-colored candle gave a delightful scent to their private nook.

"Here you are, *mes enfants*." The older woman looked down at Cyg, then at Darius. "So this is she, *oui*?" She chuckled. "You won't have it all your own way with this one, eh?" She raised her index finger and a young girl appeared and stood respectfully behind her. "Marie will be your waitress," she said. Then she clasped Cyg's hand. "I am Elise Marshall, *tante* to a very close friend of Darius's. I hope you will have every happiness."

"Thank you." Cyg stared after the woman. "Darius, what did she mean?"

Darius sighed. "Elise is like the rest of her family. They rush me." Cyg merely nodded in response. Darius ordered champagne and suggested she try the bouillabaisse.

Dinner was a delight and though Cyg wanted Darius to explain his ambiguous remark, she soon was so lost in the succulent fish stew that she forgot what she was going to say.

Champagne flowed freely through the meal, but Cyg wasn't so fuzzy she didn't notice the soulful looks the young waitresses had for Darius . . . and sometimes her.

As she was about to mention this, Darius leaned across the table and spoke. "I've thought about this so much that you would think it would be easy. It isn't." He took a deep breath and frowned at her. "And don't look so puzzled. You must have known that I would ask you . . . after our being together at Phil's." He grinned. "You must feel it's about time. So, when will you marry me?"

"What? Marry you?" Cyg was so weak, she slumped forward, her nose perilously close to her champagne glass. "I . . . I—"

"We can be married right here in Saratoga. My aunt would love to have a reception."

Cyg felt a blush spread through her body. "Why the hurry? I'm not pregnant." She glared at him. "Why marriage anyway?" She could just see his mother fainting with shame when she met her.

Darius's mellow look hardened to granite. "Why the hell not? Are you afraid to be old-fashioned?"

"Cynic." Cyg jumped up and stalked past an openmouthed *Madame* Elise.

Seven

Cyg woke up the next morning feeling like a steaming kettle with no vent. Her mind and body pulsated with an emotional hangover . . . and champagne. She closed her eyes and groaned as she recalled the skin stripping she and Darius had given each other with words after leaving the restaurant.

"Stupid, stupid." She glared at herself in the bathroom mirror. "Why did you attack him?" She jabbed at her teeth with her toothbrush. "The best defense ith attack," she lisped through her frothing mouth at her image. "No man is going to propose to me to save me . . . from whatever the hell they save you from today." She spattered the mirror with toothpaste as she expostulated. "Damn and double damn." She cleaned the glass with vicious swipes. "What if he loves you?" she spoke out loud to the reflection but didn't believe it was Cygnet Melton speaking. "How could he?" she answered back with cold logic. "His family will hate me . . . so he really doesn't love me." She put a hand up to her throbbing forehead. "Nuts," a voice deep inside said.

She pedaled to the baths in an erratic fashion,

but when the drivers honked at her, she was too down hearted to shake her fist at them.

She really wasn't sure how she did get to work all in one piece after riding on the wrong side of the road for much of the way.

Claudia blinked at her myopically. "You can't have a massage without an appointment."

"Fine," Cyg said and turned to leave the building. She was unlocking her bike again when she realized what she was doing. "Damn and triple damn. That man is driving me out of my mind." She trudged back into the building glaring at the hapless Claudia when she said, "You can't have a massage without an appointment," and kept on going until she reached the locker room.

To her great relief her first patron was unknown to her, so Cyg was able to keep conversation to a minimum, a mechanical smile and nods handling most of it.

When she went out to the desk to pick up her second assignment, Darius was there.

Cyg stared at him, mouth agape. He looked like a tractor had backed over him. His clothes were the same he had worn the night before and were badly rumpled; his hair was on end as though he had placed his finger in a light socket. His unshaven face looked like a Jack O' Lantern—swollen, with eyes like holes, "Get out of here," she bleated hoarsely.

"No." His voice was like a spike driven into oak. "Not until you explain yourself." He swayed, his one hand going to his bristly face. "I need a shave."

"You need sleep."

"That too," Darius agreed, then fixed her with a gimlet stare. "But, I'm not doing anything until you explain. And if you don't explain, I'm going to inform your aunt and mine that you are my mistress."

"Keep your voice down," Cyg hissed, watching Claudia's head come up like a bird dog's.

"Don't you tell me what to do, damn you," Darius roared, making Cyg jump and Claudia's glasses drop down her nose.

"Go home." Cyg sidled toward the double doors leading to the baths.

"No," Darius bellowed.

"I thought you were supposed to be such a gentleman," Cyg panted, her eyes rolling toward the door.

"I was . . . until I met you." Darius's face thrust forward like a bulldog's.

Cyg was going to stand her ground and shout back at him, but one look at his furious expression quailed her. She turned and ran through the double doors toward one of the cubicles, knowing that Darius could not follow her.

She closed the door, listened at it for a moment, then went to the over-sized tub and turned the spigots. She could use this cubicle for her next patron. When she heard the door bang open behind her, she spoke without looking up. "I thought I could bring my next . . ." Her voice faded when she saw the hand-tooled leather shoes next to her. "Get out of here," she squeaked looking up at Darius.

He pulled at his clothes, popping buttons on his shirt, then unzipping his pants.

"Stop! This is the women's side," Cyg begged, trying to pull his shirt up his arm again.

He shook her off like a pesty gnat and kept undressing. "You want to massage someone? Fine. I need one."

"Out of here." Cyg tugged at him, looking over her shoulder at the ajar door. "Do you want our patrons to have hysterics?" She tried to drag him toward the door.

"Get your clothes off, Cygnet, and I'll give you a massage as well." Darius didn't seem impeded by Cyg as his clothes fell to the floor one article at a time.

"What?" Cyg yelped, then lowered her voice. "Lecher . . . deviate . . . get out of here or I'll call the police."

"Call 'em." Darius turned to face her, naked. "Now about the massage." He fired the words at her like bullets.

"No." Cyg squeaked, thinking he had the most beautiful body in the world, wanting to throw herself at him and run from him at the same time.

"Yes." Darius reached for her and lifted her toward him. "So, massage me."

"Bath first," she croaked, swaying in his grip.

"Bath it is." Darius kept his hold on her as he stepped into the steamy, effervescent depths. As he started to slide down into the water, Cyg made an attempt to escape his hold. "No, you don't." Darius staggered in the slippery tub.

Sensing freedom, Cyg pushed harder against him. She hadn't reckoned on the tile floor under her feet slicking up with the splashed wetness. Darius's steel grip and lack of balance added to the leverage that tumbled her toward him.

They both sprawled into the bath, sending mini cauldrons of water spuming up and over the sides.

Cyg came up coughing and choking, unable to curse Darius as she wanted to do.

"What on earth . . .? Cyg, is that you? What are you doing? Who is . . .? Good Lord, get him out of here. How dare you bring a man into this side?" Aunt Lena's sepulchral bellow penetrated Cyg's sloshed hearing.

"Me?" She coughed. "Bring him in here?" She sputtered, incensed, trying to stand, then falling back against Darius because he hadn't released her. She glared at him through the wet swatches of hair hanging down her face. "Let me go, you . . . you vandal."

"Not until you explain." Darius flipped the wet hair out of his eyes with a shake of his head.

"I'll explain nothing." Cyg wrestled with him, pushing at him in the slick tub, their bodies roiling the water even more.

Aunt Lena stood there remonstrating with them, her voice getting strident.

Marianne walked in the door. "Gone mad, has she? Should have let me take the fussy ones."

Aunt Lena glared at her friend. "That is a *man* in there."

"Don't say." Marianne's heavy lids almost lifted. "I think this is what my granddaughter calls kinky. Wet, too."

"Don't be a fool." Aunt Lena glowered, then looked at Darius and Cyg, who were in turn glaring at each other. "Come out of there at once."

Darius stood, keeping his balance with difficulty, still holding Cyg by the hand, still nude.

"Philistine." Lena Dilson closed her eyes.

"Monster." Cyg choked, looking first at her aunt and then at Darius.

"Good body," Marianne observed, then shuffled out of the cubicle.

"I'm calling the police." Aunt Lena inhaled a deep breath, averting her eyes before turning away. "Claudia, call the *gendarmes*," she shouted as she marched from the room and down the hall.

"Will you get out of here?" Cyg spoke through clenched teeth.

"For now, but I'll be picking you up tonight . . . and if you try and run out on me, I'll handcuff you to me. I mean that." Darius grabbed a towel from the pile on the table and began to dry himself methodically. Then he put on his even more crumpled clothing.

Cyg watched him until he was fully dressed and about to leave the cubicle. "You don't scare me," she muttered to his back.

"Speak up, Cygnet." Darius looked back once. "You look more bedraggled than me now." He stalked from the room.

"Turn blue," she told the empty doorframe, then stumbled out of the tub to drip on the floor, her feet making sucking sounds in her shoes.

"In my day," Aunt Lena was shouting from the corridor," a man would marry a woman he had compromised."

Cyg winced as she listened at the half-open door.

"Good idea. Make the arrangements," Darius riposted.

Cyg heard the screen door bang, announcing Darius's departure. She sagged against the cubicle wall.

"Cyg, get dry, your next appointment is here," Aunt Lena called, bloody but unbowed.

Not much of the rest of the day registered with Cyg. She was aware that she worked her way through her appointments and her lunch. The heat of the day penetrated even the tile walls of the baths, so that much of the time she felt as though she had been immersed in the tubs herself. By quitting time at five o'clock, she was as wrung out as the towel she was squeezing dry.

The water in the employee's shower didn't seem to get cold enough and by the time Cyg had pedaled down the drive leading away from the baths, she felt almost as sweaty as she had been before she showered.

When she reached home, rivulets of water were dripping from her nose and cheeks. Her face felt scarlet hot. She wanted to fall into a vat of ice cubes.

"Hello." Darius leaned against his car.

Cyg had been looking down as she pushed her bike up the drive and hadn't seen his car. "Go home." Her voice cracked.

"Hot, darling?" Darius took the bike from her and lifted it into the rickety garage. "Take a long cold shower. I'm in no hurry."

"Fall off a mountain." Cyg pushed the words

through desert-dry lips, as she staggered up the stairs and into the bathroom.

She stripped her clothes from her body carelessly, then stood under the stream of cold water, her face lifted. She felt a draft but didn't move or open her eyes.

"Here, love, I found some lemonade in the refrigerator."

Cyg's eyes flew open and promptly filled with water. "*Aaaagh.* Get out of here." She swiped at her eyes. "My aunt will be closing the baths and be home soon. Ohhh, damn you . . . water in my mouth."

The lemonade was pressed into her hand and she was eased free of the spray.

"Drink that."

"Don't tell me what to do." Cyg took a long swallow of the tart sweet liquid, not able to stop the sounds of satisfaction coming from her throat.

"Hurry." Darius leaned down and kissed her one breast. "Ummm, very good."

"I'll send you to prison," she mumbled, taking deep breaths to steady her breathing. When she opened one eye, Darius was gone. She finished the lemonade and set the glass on the floor, so that she would remember to take it downstairs.

Dressing was easy. She reached for the coolest garment she owned, a tent affair that was strapless with ruching over the top of the bust. Then the dress flared from the bust in a circle of unpressed pleats. Every movement she made in the orange madras cotton swirled the material out from her body. Under it she wore peach-colored bikini pants. She knew that the outline of her body could be discerned, but she felt the fabric was opaque enough for decency. It was cool. With it she wore gold and coral drop earrings and cork sandals. She looped her long curling hair in an upward sweep off her neck, errant curls clinging to the sides of her head.

She sprayed cooling perfume on her neck and arms and left the room, pleased that she wasn't formally enough dressed for Darius's taste if he wanted to take her to a place like Chez Elise. She descended the stairs to the front hall.

She looked around for Darius and found him out in the back yard talking to Waldo over the fence. "Don't let him con you. If you let him out of his enclosure, he'll give you a run you'll never forget. Waldo answers only one call. Dinner." Cyg felt her smile slip sideways at the look Darius was giving her.

He pushed back from the fence, his eyes a leaf green fire as he ran them over her. "You look like orange sherbet . . . I want to bite."

"Biting on sherbet will give you a toothache," Cyg quavered, her cork soled shoes fastened to the earth as he approached her.

"I'll chance it," he whispered, lifting her toward him until their bodies were touching. His mouth began at the bone under her right ear, traveled to her left ear, then back to the middle and up to her mouth.

All Cyg's promises to herself that she would resist him melted as the roaring in her ears pushed the world away. Bare arms edged up to his shoulders, fingers touching and testing the crisp hair at his neck.

A mournful yowl pulled them apart.

"What the hell?" Darius rasped, his mouth inches from hers, his body curved over hers as his gaze searched around them.

"Waldo." Cyg managed through plastic lips. "He hates to be ignored."

"Damned fool," Darius muttered, his sardonic grin shooting from the dog on the other side of the fence then back to Cyg. "Ready for dinner?"

No, she wanted to scream at him, I'm ready for you to make love to me, and I'd like to punch you in the nose for wreaking so much havoc in my life. "Aunt Lena will probably be angry with you for some time for what you did today," she said out loud.

Darius shrugged. "I find, after all these years that I'm a Jekyll and Hyde, but only with you. I lose control with you." He frowned. "I thought I knew all the answers with women. Now I find you've written a whole new book."

"That's silly. You were married once." She could feel whip marks on her back when she said that. "Were you happy?" Blood was spilling from the open cuts.

"Maybe . . . for a while in the beginning . . . maybe not." He helped Cyg into the car after she assured him that she wouldn't need a wrap of any kind. "I usually never talk about my marriage."

"Sorry." Cyg lifted her chin.

"But I want you to know. Her name was Sabra and her family was in the export-import business in Boston. Her grandfather had gone to school with mine. Both families approved. Her cousin was my roommate at the university. We looked good together, or so we thought. We were twenty-four when we married. At twenty-five she had her first affair. She didn't want the divorce, just the freedom to bed hop in a gentile way. We divorced amicably when I told her she wouldn't get a dime from me unless she agreed to see a lawyer. The last time I saw her was two years ago . . . with her third husband. It was a relief to know that I wasn't the husband."

"You no longer loved her." Cyg felt lighter than air.

Darius reached over to take her hand. "Wrong. I had never loved her." He lifted her hand to his mouth and let his tongue caress her palm.

Cyg felt her body lift from the seat and float around the car. She blinked, trying to orient herself. "I'm not dressed for Chez Elise."

"You are dressed for anything, darling, but as it

happens I thought you might like some Italian food. We're going to Massie's."

Cyg turned sideways on her seat to face him, freeing her hand from his grasp. She ignored his chuckle. "I've been there . . . not for years, of course, but I can remember my aunt and uncle driving to Glens Falls to eat there. The food was good."

"It still is. It isn't a fancy place, but I like it there."

The car flew through the warm summer evening, the air conditioning making the ride comfortable, the tape of Barbra Streisand filling the car with poignant sound.

Somehow during the ride, Darius managed to capture Cyg's hand again. She told herself to pull free but the music and the jewel-like evening destroyed her resolve.

They parked across the street from Massie's. When they were about to cross, Darius twined his fingers in hers, fastening her to his body as he guided her to the other side.

The place was full of people in every kind of dress, from country jeans to formal black. Even though they had a reservation, there was a short wait in the bar.

It annoyed Cyg when she couldn't help noticing the looks that other women gave Darius. His tall muscular body outfitted in cream slacks, his linen jacket the same green as his eyes, his silk shirt beige and cream and open at the throat, a rope tie hanging loose under his collar.

Cyg watched him grin when a full-breasted blond rubbed against his arm. "Do you always have to wear hand-tooled leather shoes? Ostentatious," Cyg remarked, glaring at the blond.

"Huh?" Darius looked down at the light brown fine kid on his feet. "Don't you like them?"

"What does it matter what I like? Just ignore

me." Cyg lifted the Saratoga water and lime to her lips and took a long draught of the iced liquid.

Darius looked from her to the blond who hovered close by, then his smile widened as he looked back at Cyg. "Jealous, darling?" He kissed her bare shoulder.

"Conceited!" Cyg fumed. "Would you like me to pour this drink down your neck?"

"You are the greatest woman for getting me wet. I can see our life is going to be one eventful water game after the other."

Cyg's heart slipped sideways, then fell back. "Don't be an ass. We have no life."

"You're a hard woman to convince. Just remember I've been competing in a tough world for years. I'll break you down."

"Bull."

For the little more than half an hour they were there, other women stared at Darius but none approached them as the blond had done. Cyg kept a wary eye on the crowd of people and a frown ready for any woman who came too close.

When they were led into the dining room by the *maîtresse d'*, Darius put an arm around her to guide her through the barroom throng.

Cyg had to fight the urge to lean against that well-muscled form.

Darius urged her to order the Fettucine Alfredo with the side order of homemade sausage as he was doing. "The pasta is homemade, too."

"No, I think I'll have the linguine and clam sauce . . . the white clam sauce, I guess." Cyg placed the foot-long menu next to her plate.

When the waiter came, Darius ordered a tureen of minestrone along with their dinners and wine.

"I prefer New York State wine. I'm a New Yorker," Cyg responded when Darius asked her her choice. "A dry red, I think."

"I was born in New York, too," he pointed out after he indicated a New York Cabernet Sauvignon.

"Yes, but with you it's different. You've been to school all over the world."

"England and Japan, darling, and the United States."

"And your work takes you to many countries—"

"Almost any you can name. That doesn't make me any less a New Yorker than you . . . or any less a Yankee. You've got a cracker crumb . . . there." Darius leaned over, his body blanketing her from the room, and licked the crumb away.

"People will see." Cyg took a deep breath, looking left then right withoug turning her head. "You'll have us thrown out of here." She tried to act cross so that Darius wouldn't notice she was turning into a melting marshmallow. She blinked at the ice bucket standing next to Darius's chair. "Did you want the Cabernet iced?"

"It's champagne, love. We're having it with the soup."

"Oh. Nice." Cyg sipped the wine, wrinkling her nose at the bubbles.

Darius took hold of her arm. "Wait. I want to propose a toast. To us." He lifted his glass, gesturing to Cyg to do the same. Then he leaned closer, looped his arm around hers, and sipped his wine again. "Aren't you going to open your present?"

Cyg looked from him to what she had thought was wrapped Italian nuts on her plate. The square package was wrapped in silver paper.

"I'll open it for you." Darius put down his glass and tore open the silver paper, casting the silver bow aside with an indifference that made Cyg wince. She saved bows from packages. He flipped open the box and pushed it under her nose. "When will you marry me, darling?" The pear-shaped pink diamond glittered like a street lamp. "I hope you like it."

"Who wouldn't like a diamond as big as a headlight?" Cyg muttered, watching as Darius pushed it on her finger.

He frowned at the stone. "You don't like it? Would you rather choose another?"

"No . . . no, it's beautiful. But it's too much. We're not engaged." Cyg closed her fingers protectively over the ring.

"Of course, we're engaged," Darius said, then hesitated. "You were quiet tonight when I spoke of my first marriage. Does it bother you that I was married before?"

"Of course that doesn't bother me—"

"Good." He looked up. "Ah, here comes our food and our wine."

"I think I've had enough wine," Cyg muttered, trying to force herself to remove the ring. She was not able to. "In fact, I think I'm blitzed."

"What did you say, darling?" Darius poured some of the deep red liquid into another glass. "Don't worry about drinking too much. I know the effect alcohol has on you, so I'll watch your intake. I don't want you falling asleep on this special night."

"Too late. I think I'm asleep already." Cyg felt her lips crack apart in a smile when he laughed.

The dinner was delicious and though she drank some of the wine and more of the champagne, Darius made sure that she drank Saratoga water as well. Much as she wished she might just pass out of the picture, Cyg seemed to get sharper as the night went on.

Every time she tried to tell Darius that it was futile for them to be engaged, he would lean over and kiss her and whisper "Too late."

Finally Cyg tired of the game of resistance, a game she didn't want to play anyway and succumbed to what she wanted to do and be. She wanted to love Darius and belong to him.

She felt the smile on her face melt and build to gleaming fire. When she saw the slack-jawed look Darius was giving her she felt her smile widen. Tonight he would be hers! Tonight they would be engaged. She leaned over and let her lips graze his mouth, her words pushing past his lips in breathy response. "I'm having a lovely time."

"Are you, darling?" Darius swallowed, his hand coming out to grip hers where it lay on the table.

"Yes."

"God, angel, I . . ."

"Dessert, sir? Madame?" The young waiter hovered, even as *Madame* Massie bore down on him, a grim look on her face.

"Huh?" Darius looked up.

"There is no need to order just yet, sir." *Madame* took the menu from the hapless waiter, the jerk of her head telling him to retreat.

Cyg looked up at *Madame*, feeling like Wonderwoman. "A cheese board would be nice, don't you think, Darius?"

"Anything." He gazed at Cyg.

"Cheese board it shall be." *Madame* swept the menus before her, an imperious wave of her hand calling an underling.

"Where were we?" Darius asked, stroking her left hand, then kissing the ring on it.

"I was telling you that I was having a nice time."

"Yes." Darius groaned, turning her hand over and kissing the palm. "There's a place on the way back to Saratoga. I thought we'd stop there and dance, if you like."

"I like dancing." Cyg lifted her other hand to his face, feeling his body flow into hers at the touch.

"I know. Then after I thought we might stop back at my aunt's house. She's gone to visit friends and I'm staying there until her return since her housekeeper also took a vacation."

"House-sitter deluxe," Cyg murmured.

"Yes. Will you have an after-dinner drink with me there?"

"Yes. We might even play her stereo and dance there."

The cheese board came and they fed each other.

"I'm sure people think we're crazy," Cyg chuckled, accepting Brie from him.

"They know love when they see it," Darius answered, opening his mouth for a slice of apple.

"We're too old to do this." Cyg wanted to be sensible for a moment, anyway.

"You're too old. I'm not," Darius assured her.

"You're years older than I am." Cyg wished time would stand still.

"Not tonight I'm not. I've never been this young before." Darius smiled at her even as he signed the check.

"You should check the figures on the bill." Cyg's Scottish forebears spoke through her.

"Right," Darius agreed, handing the bill back to the waiter.

They walked out to the car with their arms around each other.

Cyg felt unfettered, helium light. She looked up at the sky. "Beautiful night."

"Perfect." Darius looked up and then back down at her, his mouth feathering her brow. "When I was choosing your ring, Carswell, the jeweler, spread the stones on a black velvet cloth . . ." Darius whispered, his arm tightening around her as they both looked upward. ". . . and that's the way the sky looks now, like a handful of diamonds on velvet."

"Poetic." Cyg breathed the fragrant night air.

"I may change professions. Poetry has had great appeal for me since I met you." He helped her into the car as though she were precious and breakable.

"I don't know what you do for a living anyway." Cyg sat straighter in her seat.

"Chadwick Enterprises is into a great deal. Securities, construction, large stuff like dams, building complexes. We're into banking and insurance . . ." Darius shrugged, then turned in the seat to smile at her. "I can afford to take care of you, lady, even in this tight money world."

"I didn't mean that." Cyg could feel her cheeks flushing.

"I know, but I like telling you what I do. Some of the money and holdings I inherited, but a good deal of what I own, I earned. I don't want you to think you'll be marrying a lazy man."

"Darius, about us getting married . . ." Cyg swallowed.

He took her hand and kissed the ring finger of her left hand. "We're getting married." His tongue caressed her palm before he released her and turned back to the wheel to start the engine. "Now let's celebrate."

Cyg knew she should dissuade him, that she should tell him that marriage was out, that he should take her home at once. She looked at that chiseled profile, the strong nose and chin outlined in the lights of the passing cars. He was hers for tonight!

She settled back in her seat, wriggling at the comfort of the soft leather.

Darius pushed in a tape and violins throbbed around the perimeter of the car, cocooning them in sensual rhythm.

The drive back seemed to take mere minutes, even though Cyg knew it was longer. The velvet silence between her and Darius was as intimate as any love words they might have exchanged, she was sure.

When Darius pulled into Maura Tiebold's driveway, Cyg was delighted. She wouldn't have to share Darius with anyone. They could talk to each other, touch . . . Cyg sat up in her seat, shaking her head. That man has a profound hold on me, she thought, watching him through the windshield as he came around the front of the car to help her out.

As though feeling her eyes on him, he looked back at her through the glass, his smile touching each pore of her face. When he lifted her from the car, he didn't release her. Instead, he edged her up his body, so that their eyes were level. "Sometimes it feels as though I must hold you, carry you, have you close to me."

"Too heavy," Cyg murmured, her fingertips playing over his face as though he were the most precious Stradivarius.

"A feather," he whispered back, his breath caressing her skin.

"It's nice to be so tall." She clung to his shoulder, feeling her feet hang free in a delicious abandonment of earth.

Darius held her up with one arm even as he unlocked the door. It seemed effortless to him. "As long as you like it, I'll continue to do it."

"You'll get tired."

Darius moved into the lounge area, now lit by one shaded lamp in the corner. "I can assure you, love, that I will never tire of holding you." He sank down on his aunt's settee, his well-built body filling it as though it were a chair. His lips tasted her features as though he would sculpt them with his tongue.

Cyg felt her body and spirit melt like butter in the sun. She wished all at once for a miracle glue that would fuse her to Darius for all time. "Music. Dance." A sense of survival made her speak. She had to maintain some control on herself.

"Lord, angel." Darius surged to his feet, still holding Cyg close to him. "You think of the damnedest things." He looked down at her and sighed, his smile lopsided. "Music it is, my love, and we shall dance."

When he left her to walk to the wall unit that housed the stereo, Cyg felt as though he had taken her vital organs with him. It was hard to breathe without him there: He had extracted her lungs. Blood loss was immediate; her hands and feet were cold; her insides as hollow as a drum; and her heart missing. She held up her arms to him as he turned away from the machine, a love song pulsating through the room.

"Do you want a big wedding, love?" Darius whirled her around the pegged oak floor, skirting the oval Oriental rugs scattered over its surface.

Cyg looked up at him and smothered the voice inside that told her to tell him that they would never be married. "I always thought that I would like a big cathedral wedding, but, knowing me, I probably wouldn't be able to pull it off."

"What do you mean?" Darius's mouth feathered her ear.

"I'd get scared at the ritual of it all . . . not to mention the expense. No doubt I would settle for a ladder, or a justice of the peace." Cyg swayed in his arms, loving the feel of him against her. She was home! Darius was home, haven, all love to her. Is that what women meant by marrying for security, she mused to herself, as she let her fingers pull and tug at the hair on his neck, the tactile delight rivering through her. Was love the ultimate security? Oh, God, I won't think of that, Cyg groaned to herself.

"What is it, darling? I felt you shudder. You can't be cold. Aren't you feeling well?"

"Fine. I just want you to kiss me. Now, please." Cyg pulled his head down to her, not able to control the frenzy of her movements.

Darius's arms enveloped her in the safe harbor of his passion, the feeling between them mushrooming. "I, Darius, take thee, Cygnet . . ." He kissed her deeply, leading her up the stairs and opening a door. "This is my room . . ." He spoke without taking his eyes from her. "Say it."

She knew what he wanted to hear. "I, Cygnet, take thee . . ." She sobbed, clutching at him.

He swung her up into his arms and took her to the bed, lowering his body with hers. "I belong to you Cygnet . . . and I never wanted to say that . . . nor have I ever thought it before."

He undressed her with passionate absorption, his hands and mouth lingering on her limbs.

Cygnet sensed his urgency as his body moved in supple possession over hers. The moans issuing from her throat were echoed in his hoarse cries. Need built to desire and then to consummate oneness as she felt the marrow of her bones join with his in the unending fall into sexual satisfaction. Blood cascaded through arteries as he filled her with mouth and body, pleasure like a roller coaster ride through space.

Eight

Cyg felt as though she were in the grip of a whirling dervish. At night, before going to sleep, she made grand plans to make Darius see how foolish it was for them to be engaged.

"What is the matter with him?" She faced herself in the mirror, her hand lifting in front of her to twist and turn so that the light might catch the prisms of the jewel in her ring. "It's impossible for us to marry. He'll be embarrassed after a while because I don't come from the same background." She lied even as she gripped the diamond to her chest, and an inner voice told her that Darius never would be like that. "He couldn't possibly love me . . . as much as I love him." She spat her words at the mirror, hating to verbalize that deep, hidden thought. "You are one big fool, Cyg Melton," she chided the mirror. "Since when can't you fight for what you want?" She shook her fist, then her hand fell to her side. "Yes, but the battle was never so important before." She heaved a big sigh. "He's not so big in my life . . ." She poked her tongue at the mirror. "No, not unless you count breathing in and out as important, or sleeping, eating, walking, talking, all those minor aspects of being alive." She pressed her hand against her forehead. "God, why did I let him get so close," she wailed. "You had nothing to say about it, he just took your life." She groaned.

"Cyg . . . Cyg, are you all right up there?" Aunt Lena called.

"Yes . . . yes I'm fine. You go ahead to the baths and open up, Aunt Lena. I'll be along in about half an hour," Cyg answered.

She breakfasted on slices of cantaloupe and a glass of cold milk. It only took her minutes to clean up the kitchen, then sprint back upstairs, take a quick cold shower, shampoo her hair, then brush it dry. She put on shorts and T-shirt in a burnt-orange color. She found it cooler to pedal her bike wearing the shorts even though she elicited many whistles from the motorists who passed her on the road.

When she went out to the garage to get her bike, Waldo was at the fence, snuffling at her. "Forget it, you fake. I'm not taking you for a walk now—and then have to chase you a mile to get you home again." Cyg poked her tongue at the mournful looking Basset Hound.

Waldo let out a soulful howl, which Cyg ignored as she wrestled with the lock on the garage door.

"Is that any way to treat Waldo?" Darius was behind her, his hands coming around her to unfasten the lock easily.

Cyg looked up at him, feeling moisture bead her brow, at the smile he was giving her. *With a dab of whip cream on him, I would eat him up, every bite,* she thought, turning in his arms and reaching up for him.

"God, Cygnet, don't look at me like that. We'll shock the neighbors if I make love to you here." He muttered this as his mouth coursed up and down her face. "When you purr in your throat that way, I want to thump my chest and take you into the jungle," Darius murmured, his mouth fastening to hers.

"No jungle in Saratoga," Cyg said, coming up for air. "Have to get to work."

Waldo howled again, making Cyg glare at him and Darius laugh.

"He understood you." Darius gave her another hard kiss. "Don't bother getting out the bike. I'm going to drive you. I don't like you biking down a highway. Too dangerous." He stepped around Cyg and reclosed the garage door. When he turned back to her again, his eyes went over her from head to foot. "Dangerous in many ways. No wonder Waldo was howling." His brows came together like a bridge over his nose.

"He does that because he wants me to walk him," Cyg tried to explain, feeling naked under that hot green glance.

"Too much of you is showing, my love. Lord, you have a great body. I love it," he muttered, stalking closer.

"Stop." Cyg laughed, holding up one hand to ward him off. "I'll never get to work."

"Tell me about it," Darius muttered, wrapping his arms about her. "I'm relying on telephone conferences to handle my business because I can't bear to leave town with you here. Let's get married today."

Cyg looked up at that hard-planed face, seeing the strain there, knowing that she wouldn't be telling him this morning that they mustn't marry. "We'll be married in three weeks. That's what we decided when we talked to your aunt and mine."

"I can't wait," Darius grumbled into her neck. "I want you with me every morning. I don't like waking up alone. I want you with me when I go to sleep. I'll sleep better then."

"Wanna bet?" Cyg nibbled on his chin.

Darius chuckled into her neck. "You're right. I have no plans to sleep at all the first year we're married, but I plan on being verrrrry relaxed and contented just the same," he drawled as his mouth massaged her skin.

Waldo's howl pulled them apart.

"Get your own girl, fella." Darius laughed down at the tail-wagging Basset.

"Good-bye, Waldo. Maybe I'll walk you when I come home." Cyg shut her ears to the barking that followed her down the drive. "Waldo always wants to have everything his own way," Cyg sighed as she leaned back against the chair-like seat in the Ferrari. The air-conditioned car was a balm to her heated skin. It was a treat not to have to pedal along the hot highway.

"Feeling cooler, love?" Darius glanced at her, then back to the road as Cyg nodded. "You look like orange sherbet in those shorts and shirt." His right hand came over to close on her thigh, rubbing slowly. "Such soft skin."

Cyg felt beadings of moisture on her lip that not all the air conditioning in the world could control. "Darius." She gulped as the car cruised across the highway and into the park road.

"Don't go to work today."

"Have to," Cyg said weakly, lifting his hand from her leg and holding it between both of hers.

He stopped the car in front of the baths and turned to take her in his arms. "Will you want to work after we're married?"

"What? Ah . . . maybe. No, it would be nice to have chil—" She stopped herself, wishing she could bite her tongue.

"Children?" Darius folded her close. "Wonderful. That's what I want, too. How many shall we have?"

"Twenty, maybe?" Cyg returned his embrace, but did not echo his laughter. With one last kiss, she freed herself and got out of the car.

"I'll be picking you up early. We're going to the races. Darby's Man is running and I've already placed a hundred dollars on him to win . . . in your name." He waved at her and drove away.

"I don't gamble," she whispered as she waved to him until the car was out of sight.

The day was a circus.

"These must be the ones who embarked on the Ark . . . two by two," Aunt Lena said acidly as two women walked into the reception area wearing shorts, sandals, and mink stoles over their T-shirts.

Cyg stood next to her trying to neither goggle nor giggle. The Roosevelt Baths had them all, she thought.

"Which one of you is the best?" The woman with the pinkish beehive hairdo which bobbled slightly when she walked, asked nasally. "I'm used to the best. My Stanley only wants me to have the best massoo—er."

"Sorry." Aunt Lena let her mouth stretch in a semblance of a smile. "We are masseuses. You'll have to try the other side of the baths for a masseur."

Cyg held her breath as the two women went past Claudia and through the swinging doors to the side of the baths marked MEN.

Marianne shuffled from the women's side out into the reception area, stopping next to Cyg. "No more patrons?" she wheezed, then as she heard the screeches from the men's side and the two women galloped out into the reception area, she pursed her lips together. "Twits," she said. "Bet she's got a mouse in that hair o' hers." She shuffled back into the women's side as Cyg and Aunt Lena watched the two women gesture and shout at poor Claudia.

When Aunt Lena snickered, Cyg pressed her hand over her own mouth to keep from guffawing.

"Can't have a massage without an appointment," Claudia interrupted the sputtering women.

Cyg and Lena retreated.

Cyg wasn't surprised when one of the women went to a cubicle designated as hers.

"This is a den of iniquity," the lady with the

pink hairdo told Cyg. "I intend to tell my Stanley that they have men here who expose themselves. My Stanley will sue."

Cyg plunged the flabby body under the bubbling hot water.

"*Eeeek* . . . Be careful, I could drown."

"Don't worry." Cyg noted that much of the lady with the pink hairdo's "good life-style" floated to the surface. "With diet and proper exercise, you could probably rid yourself of much of your . . ." Cyg looked at the gimlet-eyed woman and let the subject drop.

As she was leaving the room, the woman spoke again.

"I'll have you know that my Stanley thinks that my figure is perfect." Some of the effervescent water splashed into her mouth and up her nose. "And what's more . . ." She coughed. ". . . you're too skinny."

The day didn't wind down until five-thirty. By that time Cyg was a dishrag. She was glad that she didn't have the night shift at the Gideon. She had the feeling that she wouldn't have made it.

Marianne motioned to her from the bath area. "Get in here. I'm going to give you a massage for your engagement present. Lena tells me that you're going to see your man tonight. This will make you chipper."

Cyg didn't quibble. She undressed, dropped down into the filling tub, and closed her eyes. She barely wakened when Marianne urged her out of the tub and onto the massage table.

The strong capable hands of the woman flipped her like a trout on a boning board. By the time her last toe was pulled and shaken she was almost in a trance. She managed to mumble something about Darius picking her up, then she fell down into the well of sleep.

She felt something turning and pushing her." Marianne . . . is it time . . . to get dressed already?"

"Yes." Darius laughed in her ear. "You aunt has given me the keys to lock up the baths; and you most definitely *should* get dressed."

"Darius." She bubbled the word sleepily, feeling boneless. "I feel so good." She flopped her arm around his neck.

"If you keep this up, we'll make love and miss the race."

Cyg pushed herself upward, feeling that the cheek she slept on must be wrinkled and red. "Be right with you. Have to go home and get my clothes."

"No you don't. Lena gave me her key and I picked up some clothes for you." Darius both rubbed and patted her bottom. "Hurry up."

Cyg blinked herself awake and looked at the clothes that Darius had brought. A cinnamon linen suit with a crème madras cotton strapless blouse. Her shoes and bag were the same color as the blouse. He had even brought the coral jewelry she usually wore with the outfit. "How is it that you know so much about coordinating a woman's wardrobe?" Cyg called out to him in a light voice, taking deep breaths to control the snake of jealousy moving inside her.

Darius appeared in the doorway, watching her as she fastened the earring posts. "I just asked myself what would a woman who has perfect clothes sense and eye for color wear." His eyes ran over her in warm possessive assessment. "You are one beautiful lady and you always look just right . . . even in orange shorts." He picked up the shorts she was about to stuff into her duffle bag. "I think I'll always like this outfit best; but I think I want you to wear them in the privacy of our home."

Cyg felt laughter rise up in her, her body, spirit, and mind lifting at the look Darius gave her. "If I am beautiful, it's because you love me." Cyg felt her face flush. She had spoken her thoughts! She hadn't meant to say that to him! She faced him with her teeth fastened to her lower lip, her skin burning.

Openmouthed she watched his cheeks color. "Darius?"

"Darling." His voice rasped, as if it had to struggle over boulders to get out of his throat.

"I'm ready," Cyg managed to say.

"Yes." His voice was vague as his eyes touched every part of her.

She felt his look as though it were a sliver of fire running over her. "We'll be late."

He nodded, then bent his head, his mouth taking hers as though he needed it for life. "Ready?"

"Ummm."

When he put his arm around her to lead her outside, it seemed only natural to put her arm around him, too. They stayed that way even as he locked the door, put the keys into her purse so that she could give them to Lena, then unlocked the trunk to stow the duffle.

Darius only released her when he put her into the passenger seat. Even then he leaned down to kiss her again.

They didn't speak as the car traversed the roads taking them to the track. This time hordes of people clogged every entrance, cars bumper to bumper, people laughing and calling to one another in the soft summer evening.

Darius called to some and waved to many, but he didn't stop to talk with anyone on their way to his box.

Cyg felt gleeful. "This is the first time I've ever sat in these seats." She smiled up at Darius, leaning against him when he put his arm around her.

"Well, well, long time no see, Cyg, baby."

Phil Tabor's voice pumiced her skin, leaving it raw.

Cyg took long deep breaths before she turned to greet him, even as Darius was rising to his feet.

"Hello, Phil." She looked at the over-done, over-bored women with him. "How's Kim?"

"Kim? Oh . . . her. I haven't seen her in quite a while." Phil's eyes ran over her as though she were a filly for sale. "More to the point, how are you and what have . . ."

"You know my fiancée, Phil, but we don't know your companions," Darius interjected, his voice velvet-coated steel.

"Ah, yes, Darius, how are you? I thought you knew Diane Chamberlin, Janie Tukes. Ladies, Darius Chadwick."

The boredom dropped away like a discarded coat. The brunette stood straighter, her breasts thrusting at Darius.

Cyg decided that she would put a plastic bag over the brunette's head.

"Hello, Darius. We met at Schofield's . . . you know, at Southampton. I didn't recognize you for a moment. Sun in my eyes, I guess."

"Sun's almost down. You can take off your glasses now." Cyg tried to be helpful.

"Sweet." Diane threw a plastic smile in Cyg's direction. "Darius you must join us for a little party I'm having after the show at the Art Center." One taloned hand grasped Darius's wrist.

"Yes. Do join us." Janie Tukes had worked her way around to Darius's other side.

"Thanks for the invitation, but I don't know if we'll be free much in the next few weeks. We're being married two weeks from Thursday." Darius leaned down toward Cyg, his smile for her alone.

Cyg watched the horror spread over Phil's face. "You're what? You're going to marry her?" Phil choked.

Darius's head snapped up, his mouth turning rock hard, his eyes narrowing. "Is that 'congratulations' I hear from you, Phil?"

Phil stared back at him for a moment before his

eyes shifted away. "Marriage is a big step," he muttered, then jerked his head at the two women.

"Well," Diane looked annoyed. ". . . if you change your mind about coming to my party, Darius, you're always welcome."

"Good-bye." Darius turned his back, then resumed his seat next to Cyg. "Love, look, there's Darby's Man. They're leading him out now."

Cyg leaned against him, welcoming his arm around her. Maybe he didn't notice how they attempted to slight her, Cyg thought, or maybe they don't matter to him as people, but there will be other people who will matter to him and it will hurt him when they ignore me or try to pretend I'm not there. She tried to smile at him when he looked at her and kissed her nose.

"I have a feeling that you're going to bring Darby's Man good luck."

"He looks beautiful," Cyg managed, forcing all thoughts of Phil Tabor and his friends from her mind.

"No." Darius leaned over her, letting his tongue touch her ear. "You look beautiful. He looks ready to run."

"You're a nut."

"This nut is nuts about you."

"More poetry?" Cyg smiled at his face so close to her own. "Why Mr. Chadwick, suh, you'll turn my head."

"That's my plan. I'll get you so drunk on my poetry, that I'll be able to run away with you . . . today."

"Anyone would think you were anxious to tie the old millstone of marriage around your neck." Cyg lifted her left hand and rubbed the stone on her third finger against his face.

"I have never . . . but never wanted anything so much in all my life as I want that," he whispered, the call to colors not making him turn away from her. "You, too?"

"Me, too!" She was not able to lie to him about it.

At the shout "They're off" Darius turned toward the track, his arm still tight around Cyg.

Before she knew it, she was standing, shouting, screaming for Darby's Man.

As though the horse could hear her, the animal seemed to make a break through the pack on the far turn and sprint through the middle.

"Look . . . Oh, Darius, look at him." Cyg felt as though she were losing oxygen. She could hear Darius chuckle beside her as she climbed onto the seat, holding onto his shoulder. "Come on, Darby . . . Darby, you can do it."

Neck and neck, he and another horse came around the turn into the home stretch as the crowd roared and screamed its approval.

"He'll do it, he'll do it." Cyg pummeled Darius's shoulder as he held her on the seat.

Dancer's Folly beat Darby's Man by a nose at the wire.

Cyg pointed an accusing arm toward the track, mouth agape in disbelief. "Darius," she moaned, sinking down from the chair into his arms. "He lost. It isn't fair."

"He ran a beautiful race," Darius said in a soothing tone while folding her close, unmindful of the disgruntled persons around them tearing up the tickets.

"He should have won." Cyg clutched Darius to her.

"If this is what you do when our horses lose, I'll arrange to have all of them come in a close second." Darius chuckled into her ear, then leaned back to look at her, the gleam in his eyes going over her like a velvet cloak.

"Darius, you're putting on a show for all of the owners, I see," Diane Chamberlin called over from the box she shared with Janie and Phil Tabor.

Darius never looked away from Cyg. She shot a

quick glance toward the other box and intercepted Phil's sardonic smile.

They stayed for the other races, but Cyg found it hard to concentrate on the sleek thoroughbreds. Her nerve ends seemed to pick up Phil's every snicker and the laughter of the two women. Had Phil told them that he considered her and Kim "girls" that he used for entertainment purposes? Cyg winced as though her thoughts were needles through her skin.

Darius turned, putting down his binoculars. "What is it, darling? Had enough?"

Cyg swallowed at the concern on his face, wanting to tell him that she wanted to run and hide and take him with her; that she wanted to be a hermit with him on top of a mountain; that dead center in the Mojave Desert would be fine with her if he were there. "Let's watch until the end." She felt her smile slip sideways when he nodded and picked up the glasses again.

When it was over and many people approached Darius, he pulled her into the circle of one arm and began introducing her as his fiancée, his voice deep with pride. "Yes, Jim, we'll be married in just under three weeks," Darius said for the umpteenth time, his grin widening every time someone said "Lucky dog" or "Good for you, she's lovely."

Darius refused all offers of get togethers much to Cyg's relief, but it amazed her when he told everyone that he was turning down their invitations because he wanted to be alone with her.

When they were at last in the car, Darius reached over to squeeze her thigh gently. "I wish my aunt was still out of town. I need to make love to you."

"I need it, too, darling," Cyg whispered, feeling the blood course through her body at a greater speed when Darius looked at her.

"Do you think you'll mind remaining in bed for three months after we're married?"

"Only three months?" Cyg purred, moving as close to him as the gearbox would permit. Then she straightened in her seat. What was the matter with her? She was beginning to act as though she would be able to keep him, that she would be able to marry him, when all reason told her that it was impossible.

Darius parked in Lena Dilson's short driveway and turned to look at her. "Where can we be alone? I can't hold you in this damn car."

Cyg couldn't help laughing at his glowering look. "No doubt this car was designed by a father whose daughter was dating a rake like you."

"Rake? Me?" Darius leaned over and pushed a button and the seat shot further back, with almost the same motion he lifted Cyg from her seat and hoisted her across the gears and into his lap. "Where did you get that old-fashioned word, lady mine?" His lips played over her face.

"Well . . . maybe libertine would be better," Cyg murmured, her hands exploring his face as though she would X ray him with her fingers. Electricity charged up her arm, down again, back into Darius, then through her again.

"God, woman, having you on my lap is dynamite to my libido." He grinned as she pressed her face against him. "But you can feel that, can't you, darling?"

"Yes." Her voice was muffled into his neck.

"I tell you now that I never thought it possible to feel this way about anyone." He urged her face free of his neck so that he could see her in the dim light from the dashboard. "At night, when I've just left you, I find myself imagining what our children will look like. . . . What we'll look like on our fiftieth wedding anniversary. What's even crazier I find those thoughts totally erotic." He interspersed his words with kisses, his mouth edging the front of her dress downward. "Did I tell you that I love your breasts?"

"Maybe." Cyg's thoughts were like mashed potatoes as his mouth took hold of one nipple.

"I want to make love to you. I'm long past necking in a car," Darius muttered, as he shifted her body in his arms so that he could caress her other breast. "On the other hand, it sure beats not holding you at all."

Cyg gripped him with desperate hands, not even wanting to say good night to him, her tongue touching the roughening beard of his face. "Sometime . . . I want to shave you myself," she mused.

"How about every morning? Lord, I'll have to move my office to our house. I won't have the strength to leave you."

She felt his mouth widen in a smile under her hand. "What's so funny?" she asked, cuddling closer, loving the feel of his muscular thighs under her hips.

"I'm going to make you my special assistant in the office. That way I'll keep you with me all the time." His hands tightened on her waist. "Except, of course, when we have our family. Then, I will work at home."

"You won't like me when I'm misshapen." She didn't listen to the voice that told her that she would never be pregnant with his child.

"You will never be misshapen. You'll just get more beautiful. I'll still make love to you when you're ninety."

"I want that in writing," Cyg cooed.

Darius hooted with laughter, then groaned. "Darling, you have to go in . . . or we have to find a motel. As it is, I may have to take a bath in ice cubes when I get back to the Gideon."

Cyg leaned against him as he opened the car door and eased her around and through the opening.

Instead of putting her down as Cyg figured he would, he levered himself out of the car still holding her, then carried her to the door. He allowed her to slide down his body, then they stood there, their bodies fitting like two pieces of a puzzle. "I've revised my opinion on car necking. It has some good points." His voice was guttural against her neck. "Sleep tight, lady mine, and dream of me."

"Uh-huh." Cyg slipped inside the door, then stayed there until she heard his car coast down the drive, Darius starting the engine when he was on the road.

She did dream of Darius all night, and of him making love to her when she was ninety.

She woke feeling refreshed and happy, no unhappy thoughts intruding through breakfast or while she dressed and straightened her room.

Again, as she went out to get her bike, Darius was there, leaning on his car. "I thought you had to catch up on work this morning." Cyg could feel her smile stretching across her face, happiness filling her at the sight of him.

His eyes scored her up and down as he approached her. "Turquoise shorts today, is it? God, woman, your body should be registered with the police department." His kiss was hard, long, and searching.

"You might get fired from your job for loafing?" Cyg managed to ask.

"I should be fired. Thank God, I'm the boss. I find that I can better concentrate on work if I call in what I want done, then come and see you." He led her to the car, speaking to a mournful-looking Waldo at the same time, then helped her into the car with a warm kiss on her ear. "I haven't worked out how I'm going to take you to work with me after we're married, but we'll think of something." He shrugged.

Cyg laughed. "Fool. You can't take me to work with you."

He shot a smile her way. "Maybe, but I don't know how I'll be able to leave you home. The more

I dwell on it, the more attractive working at home becomes."

Darius surprised her by coming into the baths with her. Claudia looked up at once.

"You can't get a massage without an appointment."

"I have an appointment." Darius leaned over the desk until he was close to Claudia.

"Oh." She looked flustered.

"What did he say?" Aunt Lena said as she came out into the reception area.

"You do?" Cyg looked at his body and for the first time in her life wished to be a man so that she could be the one to give Darius his massage.

"Good body." Marianne spoke out of the side of her mouth, without once looking up as she shuffled past.

"Yes." Darius turned to Cyg and winked. "We have a command performance with Aunt Maura and her friends at the Art Center tonight." He looked at Lena, missing the tightness on Cyg's face. "She called you, didn't she, Mrs. Dilson?"

"Yes, she did." Aunt Lena took a deep breath. "And I called my brother and sister-in-law about coming down for the engagement party she is planning for Saturday evening. They said that they would come."

"Mom and Dad are coming to Saratoga?" Cyg whirled to face her aunt.

"Yes, and they were very disappointed that you haven't called and told them about your boyfriend and your coming marriage," Aunt Lena lectured.

"Ashamed of me, darling?" Darius's voice was teasing steel.

"No need to be. Great physique." Marianne shambled past on her way to the linen closet.

Cyg glared at the woman who never bothered to look at her. Darius laughed. "Marianne, are you coming to our wedding?"

Marianne stopped dead, her drooping eyelids lifting a fraction. "Dunno. Am I invited?"

Aunt Lena tried to signal Darius who seemed impervious to her waving hand.

"Consider yourself invited . . . by me . . . the groom."

"Fine. I'll be there. Wear my feathered hat." Marianne disappeared into the linen closet.

Aunt Lena closed her eyes and sighed. "She'll talk out loud all during the service and no doubt describe in detail how great sex can be if you keep in shape by coming to the baths." Aunt Lena sucked in gulps of air and turned away.

"She won't?" Cyg asked in a reedy voice, torn between horror and laughter.

"Will, too," Aunt Lena promised, disappearing from the reception area as Homer Weeds, a masseur, came from the men's side of the baths and approached Darius.

"You Mr. Chadwick?" Homer inquired.

Cyg stared at the masseur, fascinated. Homer did not look as though he had grown. It seemed to Cyg as though someone had stacked him like hay bales. His keg of a head was balanced on T-shaped bales that were his body. They, in turn, were placed on the tree stumps that were his legs. Though he was only past middle height, Homer was an awesome sight.

"Yes, I'm Chadwick." He turned back to Cyg, taking her fully into his arms and kissing her with a slow absorption that turned her legs to softened cheese.

"I . . . I have to work at the Gideon for an hour tonight," she panted.

He ran his index finger down her nose. "I remember. I'll wait in the lobby for you and do some work."

"You could wait in your room."

He shook his head. "And not be able to lift my head and see you? No way."

Cyg couldn't have stopped her smile if her mouth had been taped.

Darius leaned down to her. "Don't do that . . . unless you want me to carry you out of here to some secluded spot, lady." He gave her one quick kiss and followed the shorter man through the swinging doors.

Marianne came out of the linen closet. "Made love to you, did he? Ought to be able to handle yourself better." She paused for a moment, pulling air noisily up her nasal passages. "Course, if it was me, I'd of drug him out to a field somewheres." Marianne shuffled past Cyg into the women's side of the baths, oblivious to the murderous look Cyg was giving her.

The day was crazy. Cyg had a woman who giggled the whole time she was in the baths, her New York City high-rise voice penetrating to every corner of the building.

"Wait'll I tell my friend, Ceil, that I took one o' these. She'll die, honest to Gawd, she will." She stopped giggling for a moment to fix Cyg with a gimlet eye. "This is very eratic, ya know. Very."

"*What?*" Cyg struggled to lift the flaccid woman from the tub and direct her onto the table.

"Ceil sez that hot tubs and jacuzzis are eratic . . . You know sexy, like they say, that new word for it, you know," Mrs. Degnan ("Call me Liz, hon, everyone does") explained patiently.

"Ohhh, erot—eratic . . ." Cyg nodded, flipping the woman onto her front. "Now I understand."

"Well, I thought you would. Girls like you know all about that stuff."

"Girls like me?" Cyg asked in measured tones, her hands poised above Mrs. Degnan ("Call me Liz," etc.). "What does that mean?"

Mrs. Degnan shrugged under the white sheet.

"Well, you know . . . Messin' around with all those guys when you give them a massage."

"Mrs. Degnan, the Roosevelt Baths have masseurs for the men, and masseuses for the women." Cyg spoke through her teeth, her hands coming down in a karate chop on Mrs. Degnan's gluteus maximus.

"*Owwww* . . . Hey, are you supposed . . ."

"It's a fact of life that the body sometimes suffers when it is sadly out of shape, Mrs. Degnan." Cyg pummeled Mrs. D from thigh to calf and back again.

Before the woman could do much more than whisper "Oh," Cyg flipped her onto her back and started the toe jerk on the front.

Mrs. Degnan lifted her head, a ferret look to her face. "But on the sly, after hours . . . isn't it true that you young ones— *Owww* . . . my leg. You're squeezing . . ."

"Really?" Cyg felt a crocodile smile stretch her lips.

"Anyway, you can tell me." Mrs. D leaned up from her prone position, her eyes beady and watchful.

Cyg took one of the hot towels from the rack and wrapped it none too gently around Mrs. D's face. "Time for your nap, Mrs. Degnan."

"*Umphle . . . Mumphle . . . Umphle . . .*" Mrs. Degnan's eyes popped over the top of the towel.

Cyg held her breath until she was out of the cubicle and in the compartive coolness of the corridor. "That . . . woman . . ."

Nine

Cyg wasn't at all nervous with Darius in the lobby of the Gideon Putnam during her shift at the desk. It delighted her to have him gazing at her whenever she looked at him, which was often. The power that generated between them awed her. There was no need for words: Her skin came alive at a command from Darius.

The nervousness didn't come until he dropped her at home, telling her he would return for her when he was dressed. Then they would call for his aunt before going to the Art Center.

Cyg whirled in front of the mirror, liking the apricot color of the silk Thirties-type dress that she had found in the *avant garde* boutique in the Village. The dress relied for style on the form of its wearer, the clinging bias-cut gown having spaghetti straps with a swirl of natural pleats at the knee line. The material was filmy enough to demand a slip of the same color, but Cyg did not wear a bra, her firm breasts giving the dress its curving top outline.

Following the Thirties motif, she parted her hair in the middle and, by wetting and combing, encouraged the natural curl in her hair to wave backward from her forehead to a tight bun at the nape of her neck.

The jewelry she wore was coral. Long pieces of coral swung against her cheeks to her jawbone. No necklace interrupted the expanse of neck, chest, and the provocative swell of bust from the low-cut dress. Her engagement ring gleamed with an even deeper pink light against the backdrop of the apricot silk.

When Cyg slipped the salmon pink leather slides on her feet and reached for the old-fashioned lamé cosmetic bag that she had found in a tiny store on Third Avenue, she stood in front of the mirror taking deep breaths. "You just have to make it through this evening," she muttered at her mirror image. "Then tomorrow . . . or the next day, or the next . . . find a time to tell Darius that marriage won't work." She pressed the flat of her hand against her stomach, trying to suppress the growls coming from there. "I'll eat a soda cracker."

The door swung open wider. Darius stood there, staring at her, his eyes going over her from head to foot. "Your aunt told me to come up and hustle you." He spoke in an offhand way, still looking at her. He fixed on her hand over her stomach. "Tummy upset, love?"

"No," she croaked, feeling the heat in his eyes course over her.

"You're too beautiful to take out in public," he murmured. "No bra . . . your beautiful breasts . . . slender hips and thighs. You look like an apricot angel." He opened up his arms.

Cyg knew her feet only touched the floor once as she glided forward against his body. When he embraced her, she knew she was home.

"I would like to take you to bed . . . not to the Art Center," Darius mumbled into her neck.

"Sounds good to me." Cyg let her arms twine around his neck.

Daris groaned, putting his hands at her waist and pushing her away from him.

"Don't want me?" Cyg pouted, loving the feel of

his shaven face as her finger coursed down his chin.

"Cygnet, when we're married, you can tease me all you want . . . but not now. Not with your aunt waiting downstairs."

She laughed, feeling free, and put her arm through his. He was hers for one more night! She was going to enjoy and delight in every moment.

Aunt Lena was waiting in the downstairs hall, resplendent in beige with brown accessories. She smiled up at Darius as he preceded Cyg down the narrow stairs, his hand behind him holding Cyg's. "I thought I might have to sound a siren to get you both down here. My, my Cyg, you do look pretty."

"She's beautiful," Darius agreed.

Cyg passed him and went over to her aunt and kissed her cheek. "You look pretty classy yourself, lady."

"Yes, I think I do, too." She grinned as Darius laughed. "You look pretty sexy yourself, Mr. Chadwick. If someone had told me that a man could wear a Hunter green silk suit and look masculine I would have pooh poohed, but he does, doesn't he Cyg?"

"He's beautiful," Cyg cooed, delighted when Darius blushed.

"Well, I wouldn't say that." Lena winked at Cyg, grinning openly at Darius.

"Come on you two, time to go." Darius shepherded the women out the door, a sheepish smile lighting his face as they teased him.

Cyg stopped outside staring at the Rolls Royce Brougham in the driveway. Waldo and his owner were both at the fence.

"Nifty car," Mr. Brownell observed, his pipe clutched in his mouth.

Waldo howled at Cyg, who glared back at the dog.

"You look nifty, too, Lena." Mr. Brownell pulled his pipe from his mouth and tapped it against his shoe. "'Bye. C'mon Waldo. Walky walk."

The Basset Hound ambled after his master.

"Walky walk. Look how that dog has him fooled." Cyg fumed as Darius handed her into the front seat of the car after closing the back door when Lena was seated.

"Oh, my, Darius, toot the horn. There's May Smitts. I want to wave to her." Lena chuckled as Darius slowed and she waved to Birch Street's greatest gossip. "Thank you, dear. Drive on."

"I think Aunt Lena is getting to like the Rolls," Darius whispered as he pulled gently at Cyg's arm to urge her closer to him.

"Serve you right if she makes you chauffeur her all over Saratoga Springs." Cyg tried to look severe, but she couldn't push the smile from her face.

When they picked up Maura, she and Lena began to chatter at once, almost ignoring Darius and Cyg.

He made sure that he dropped the older women at the front entrance of the Art Center, but Cyg shook her head and stayed with him while he parked. She didn't want to be separated from him for a moment until she had to.

They walked hand in hand the length of the parking lot, neither one taking notice of the people around them.

"Going to ignore us, Darius?" Diane Chamberlin caroled across the lot. "We missed you at the party the other night. You, too . . . ah . . ."

"Yes." Janie Tukes agreed, pushing out her chest so that her breasts almost tumbled free of the strapless dress she was wearing, "We missed you."

Cyg frowned at the two women before looking past them and seeing the mocking smile on Phil Tabor's face as he stood with several people who were looking their way and muttering to each other.

"Hello, Darius. Cyg, you remember Will Davis . . . Mark . . . Binny . . . Trey . . . Sarrow." Phil reeled off even more names, but Cyg didn't hear. She was too busy trying not to wriggle with discomfort at the looks she was getting from the people with Phil.

"Maybe you could come to the house, Dar, after . . ." The man called Will Davis shrugged in Cyg's direction.

"We're busy," Darius snarled, then took Cyg's arm and frog marched her toward his aunt and hers who were waiting at the entrance.

Several of the people behind them hurried forward to speak to Maura Tiebold, giving a cool acknowledgment when she introduced Lena Dilson as Darius's aunt to be.

"Have you met our lovely Cyg, who is to marry Darius very soon?" Maura waved Cyg forward, not seeming to notice how tight-faced both Darius and Cyg were at the moment. "We're having the reception at the Gideon Putnam . . . for several close friends and family. Aren't we, Lena?"

Aunt Lena beamed back at her friend and nodded.

Cyg stared openmouthed at the two women, then sidled closer to her aunt. "I didn't know about this." She nudged her aunt, speaking out of the side of her mouth.

"Lovely, isn't it?" Aunt Lena murmured, her face having a sheen to it.

To Cyg's jaded eye it seemed as though her serene aunt had taken on the properties of a religious zealot. "How many?" she breathed, fearing the answer.

"Two or three hundred, I think." Aunt Lena lifted Cyg's nerveless hand and patted it.

"No."

"Yes, dear, it should be quite lovely, don't you think?"

"No."

"I knew you'd be pleased." Aunt Lena moved away from Cyg and toward Maura as the other woman expounded on the coming nuptials.

"Does a big ceremony bother you, love?" Darius ignored the others.

"Yes. Second marriage." Cyg could feel her mouth opening and closing like a fish.

"My second, your first, love. And I think the bride dictates how the wedding is run." Darius tried to soothe her.

"Ladder!" Cyg implored Darius.

"I'd like to elope, too, darling, but Aunt Maura has her heart set on a splash for us. She even invited her many friends in government. A few congressmen, a couple of senators . . . ah . . . let me see . . ." Darius thought as he led her into the lovely lobby of the Center.

"Please God, not the president," Cyg babbled, clutching at Darius.

"I think she called him." Darius held the door for her, then frowned when Cyg stared glassy eyed at the wall. "Come on, love."

"She . . . called . . . the . . . president . . . of . . . the United States of America?"

"Yes." Darius ushered the older women down to their seats while still holding on to Cyg.

She sat when the others sat; stood when the others stood. She applauded when they did, but she did not know what happened on the stage.

At intermission, they mingled with the hordes of people stretching their legs and having a cool drink.

Cyg took the iced white wine that Maura insisted they all drink. She lifted her hand to the toast Darius's aunt made but she didn't know what was said.

The crowd swelled and parted. She found herself separated from Darius for a moment.

"Aunt Maura is inviting me to the wedding." Phil spoke close to her ear. "Lucky girl, Cyg Melton. You really played your cards right with old Dar. I never knew a cannier guy in my life, but you landed him and his maximillions." He stepped in front of her and lifted his glass in salute.

Cyg blinked and focused on the man in front of

her. "Darius loves me. Isn't that enough for you to wish us both happy?" She pushed the words through cardboard lips.

"You don't fit in, Cyg. Call girls don't marry men of our class." Phil's smile turned into a snarl.

"You're wrong on one count, Phil." Cyg felt temper build like lava inside her. "You have no class. You're a creep." Cyg tipped her glass down the front of his frilled evening shirt, watching with clinical interest as he leaped backward, spilling more liquid from his own glass.

"Damn you . . ." His voice had a reedy threat, even as he looked around him and tried to mask his anger.

Darius was there, pushing against Phil's chest. "What the hell are you saying. Hey, what's wrong with you? Your shirt's wet." Darius shook his hand, before he gripped Phil's shirtfront again. "Stay away from Cygnet. I told you that once before. I won't say it again." He flung Phil from him, paying no attention to the few people who had noticed the disturbance.

"Come on, darling, the interval is over." Darius looked down at her. "Where's your wineglass?"

"Phil took it . . . the wine that is." Cyg grinned, feeling relaxed for a moment.

Darius studied her, then smiled. "You can explain that to me when we're seated. I can guess from the gleam in your eyes that you managed Phil on your own."

"I did . . . yes." She took hold of his arm, pressing close to him.

The rest of the show was a little more enjoyable for Cyg and though she missed the thread of the first act she was able to relax through the second.

When they dropped the older women at home, Darius told her that he was taking her for a drive.

They drove for some miles. "There . . . up ahead . . . is the entrance to the battlefield where the famous Battle of Saratoga was fought." Darius pulled over to the side of the road. "But tonight I'm not interested in history lessons." He reached across the seat and pulled her toward him. "I love this Rolls. We can neck without anything coming between us." His mouth invaded hers.

For a moment Cyg had the feeling that they were whirling in space as he kissed her, then she realized that he had lifted her across his lap and was holding her tight to his body.

"Besides I have something for you." Darius reached into his pocket and pulled a box from it.

"You mustn't give me so many things." She gasped as he opened the case and lifted teardrop earrings from the blue velvet bed.

"These were my grandmother's and, though she was alive when I married the first time, she told my Aunt Maura that I was not in love and so she wouldn't give them to me. Aung Maura told me that story when I came into possession of the jewels on my grandmother's death." Darius fitted his mouth to hers again. "I know she would want you to have them."

"Darius . . ." Cyg felt tears clog her throat. "I . . . I never cry." She gasped, lifting her hand to touch his cheek.

"You can cry, scream, laugh, growl . . . or anything you choose, my love. When we're married, I'm going to make a career of getting you everything you've ever wanted."

"Leave it to you to pick an easy job," Cyg babbled into his neck, her one hand still clutching the jewel box. "You're all I've ever wanted," Cyg confessed, feeling as though a boulder had lifted from her body. She had needed to tell him that!

His body tensed under hers, his hands trembled slightly as they caressed her. He leaned back from her a little. "Do you mean it?" His voice was barely audible.

She nodded, her index finger tracing the outline of his face. "Oh, yes, I mean it. I—" She stiffened, her body crouching close to him. "What's that sound . . . like a baby crying?" She tightened her grip on him when Darius made to put her aside. "No, you can't go out there. Lock the doors. Oh, Darius, there it is again. Is it a baby?"

He unfastened his arms from her neck, making soothing sounds all the while. "Don't worry. I think it must be an animal of some kind."

Cyg watched him take the flashlight from the glove compartment, open his door, and step outside the car. She moved across into his seat, determined to follow him if there was trouble.

"Easy, easy now," Darius said. Then he bent and lifted something into his arms.

"It's a cat." Cyg was openmouthed. "It looks terrible. What happened to it?" She moved further back onto the seat to allow Darius to reenter the car, carrying the wet, bedraggled creature.

"I think someone tried to drown her. She's obviously pregnant." Darius put the cat on the seat between them, then gave Cyg a rueful smile. "So much for necking on a country road."

"Poor baby . . ." Cyg crooned, scooping up the wet creature and talking to it.

When they reached Aunt Lena's house, Darius helped her settle the cat on some old towels in the kitchen with a bowl of milk and corn flakes.

"I didn't know cats ate corn flakes," Darius mused, nuzzling Cyg's neck as they stood in the doorway.

"Beggars can't be choosers. Maxine will love them." Cyg opened her lips on his mouth, feeling the pleasurable thrust of his tongue.

"God, I can't take much more of this. We have to get married."

Cyg thought of what he said as she looked at the cat one last time, then went upstairs to wash and go to bed. If she was going to leave Darius, she should do it soon . . . tomorrow.

Twice in the night she woke with her face and hands itching. She could feel swelling on her cheeks. She must be coming down with something, she told herself muzzily, then she fell asleep again.

When she woke at six, her throat was dry and her skin was itching fire. She staggered to the bathroom and looked at herself in the mirror. "Good Lord." The words fell out of the hole in a pumpkin face. "I look like a pink basketball. What on earth . . . ?"

She was still tying her bathrobe around her when she went down the stairs to the kitchen.

Aunt Lena was there petting Maxine. She turned and looked at Cyg and winced. "Why did you take such a chance when you know you're allergic to them?"

"Allergic? I forgot." Cyg pressed her hand against her tender skin and flinched. She tried to smile at her aunt, but her mouth wouldn't stretch past a grimace. "Maxine's cute, isn't she? I always liked silver tabbies. They're so smart."

"Smarter than you, I think." Aunt Lena picked up the cat, towels and all. "We'll give Maxine a room in the garage for the time being." She jerked her head at Cyg. "You get upstairs and—"

The phone rang.

Cyg waved her aunt away and answered it.

"Cygnet? Darling? I think you should put the cat outside. I just remembered you told me that you were allergic . . ." Darius's voice was crisp.

"Too late, Maxine got me."

"You sound as though you have marshmallows in your mouth."

"Sadist. Darius, don't come over today. I'm going to stay in bed all day." Cyg knew that she would take this chance to leave Saratoga and Darius. She hung up the phone before she howled.

Aunt Lena returned to the house, washing her

hands at the sink. "Why aren't you in a baking soda bath? That's the—"

"Aunt Lena, I'm leaving today. I can't marry Darius, knowing he thinks I'm a call girl." Cyg gulped air.

"Stop that. He loves you. A blind man could see it," Lena snapped.

"Did you see how his friends acted last night?"

"They are fools . . . and I think Darius shares that opinion." Aunt Lena's voice was as tart and crisp as a September apple.

"He can't turn his back on all his friends," Cyg stated, her mouth dry. "Phil Tabor has spread the word about me. I know it."

"The man's an ass." Lena Dilson seemed to swell. "And I think you should fight for your reputation . . . not run away."

Cyg Melton stared at her aunt. "You think that I wouldn't rather stay and fight? That I wouldn't rather punch Phil Tabor in the eye and tell him to go to hell? Well, I would do that, if I didn't think that Darius would be the victim, eventually. I am not going to be the cause of a lifetime of discomfort for him. I love him too much."

"Then fight for him." Lena shook her finger in Cyg's face.

"I am fighting, Aunt Lena . . . in my own way." Cyg turned and marched up the stairs to her room.

She took a long hot bath in baking soda. That alleviated much of the itching. The ice bag Aunt Lena had given her took down some of the swelling. She knew she wouldn't have to get any antihistamines because as long as she stayed away from the cat, the swelling would go down.

It surprised her to find Aunt Lena in the kitchen when she went back downstairs, dressed and with one suitcase in her hand. "Today isn't your day off, is it?"

"Did you want your mother and father to arrive for a wedding that wouldn't take place?"

"I forgot." Cyg pressed her hand against her mouth.

"Seems to me you're getting scatterbrained." Aunt Lena glared at her, arms akimbo.

"Thank you for all you've done for me. I'll call you when I get settled." Cyg tried to smile but her mouth wobbled. She put her arms around her aunt and sucked in deep breaths.

"Get going." Aunt Lena pushed back from her. "Have to get to work." She walked into the bathroom off the kitchen and closed the door.

Cyg frowned at the closed door for a moment, then shrugged and went outside.

Waldo was barking and trying to climb up the fence. Maxine was sitting in the open door to the garage, cleaning her paws and watching the jumping, howling dog. She looked bored.

"At last somebody has arrived who will drive you crazy, Waldo, instead of the other way around," she murmured, looking from the dog to the cat but not getting near either one.

"You don't look too swollen."

"*Ahhhh*," Cyg yelled, whirling to face Darius who stood just behind her. "Are you trying to give me a heart attack?"

"I'll do more than that if you ever try to leave me again. No more games, Cygnet." His lips looked like two steel rods pushed into granite.

She opened her mouth but no sound came out. She sniffed, positive she would be able to smell the sulfur coming off his body. She had never seen Darius's color fluctuate from white to red and back again. Was there smoke coming from his distended nostrils?

He leaned forward.

Cyg took one step backward. "I'm not afraid." Her voice had a reedy sound. "You're not the type to strike a woman."

"That's right. I'm not. I've never struck a woman in my life, but you damn well deserve a good paddling." He shot the words at her like hot rivets.

Cyg had the feeling that she should bob and weave to avoid what he was saying. It was like standing in the middle of a rifle range to talk to him when he was in a rage. "I wanted to save you from being embar—"

"*Shut up!*" Darius roared, making Waldo stop jumping and barking and cower next to the fence. Maxine hightailed it up the door of the garage to crouch on the roof, hissing and spitting.

"*Ahhhh!*" Cyg yelped, taking two steps backward.

"Don't you ever . . ." Darius huffed, shaking trees and bending bushes with his fury, ". . . intimate to me that you are an embarrassment to me, that you don't fit in with my friends as your aunt told Maura."

"Lena—" Cyg closed her eyes when Darius seemed to swell.

"Yes, she damn well did call my aunt, and that's the only thing saving you from being leg-shackled until our wedding in four days' time. Until then, I am not letting you out of my sight. Is that clear?"

"I think it's clear in Albany even!" Cyg muttered, watching Waldo try to dig his way into Mr. Brownell's potato garden.

"Cygnet!" Darius bellowed.

Cyg watched Maxine's hair stand straight out, as she showed all her teeth. "Waldo is digging a coal mine. Would you stop yelling? Please?"

"Then give me your word, you won't try anything like this again," he snarled, his threatening vibrato making Waldo dig faster and some crows rise up from the power lines.

"Darius, you don't—"

"Your word, Cygnet." The words bombed out of his mouth, scattering some morning doves.

"My word . . . my word . . ." Cyg hastened to speak as Mr. Brownell came out on his back porch.

"Not that I'm letting you out of my sight anyway.

I'm not." He gripped her arm above the elbow. "Is this all your clothes?"

"Clothes? No. I left some . . ." Cyg was whirled around and almost dragged back into the house. She glared at her Aung Lena, who leaned against the refrigerator, a satisfied smile on her face. "Traitor," Cyg said.

"Foolish girl." Aunt Lena frowned at her, then beamed at Darius. "I feel much better about Cyg's future knowing you'll be around to get her out of the scrapes she gets into."

"Scrapes? Me?" Cyg pushed out her jaw.

"Now she looks just like her father."

Darius studied Cyg. "Does she?" Then he looked back at her aunt. "I'm taking Cyg to stay at my aunt's house until the wedding. My aunt is taking over my suite at the Gideon."

"Not bloody likely," Cyg expostulated. "I'm not . . ."

Darius bent, pulled Cyg's one arm forward, then caught her over one shoulder, fireman's carry style. He straightened and Cyg dangled, front and back over his shoulder. "Aunt Lena, Cygnet is getting difficult again. Would you mind bringing the rest of her clothes to my aunt's house?"

"Put me down, you sadist . . . deviate." Cyg felt sure she would have a bloody nose, suspended upside down as she was.

"Not that she needs many clothes. I've arranged for Charine's of New York to have clothes sent in Cygnet's size."

"Robber baron, smuggler, hijacker. I won't wear your clothes . . ." Her voice was getting nasal as her nose filled with fluid. "I'll sue you."

Lena Dilson laughed.

"And I'll sue my aunt, traitor that she is." Cyg flailed at Darius's back with her fist but it had no effect. She lifted her head as he carried her out the door and to the car. Aunt Lena followed, a smug look on her face. "I'll send you to Attica Prison," Cyg croaked.

"Don't worry, Mr. Brownell," Aunt Lena caroled. "Cyg is going to stay at her boyfriend's house for a few days. Hello, Waldo, dear. What are you doing in that hole in the potato garden? Good heavens, the cat is on the garage roof."

"Didn't know Cyg drank, Lena." Mr. Brownell tapped his pipe on the fence, twisting his head so that he could look at Cyg.

Cyg lifted her head again. "I am not drunk! I am being abducted."

"Cyg, child, shame on you for getting into my cooking sherry again," Aunt Lena tutted, shaking her head at Mr. Brownell and whistling to the cat to come down from the garage.

"Face is all swollen from drink, girl," Mr. Brownell admonished as Cyg was flung right side up and shoved into the front seat of the car. "Stay off the hard stuff, girl."

Before a fuming Cyg could move, Darius was around the car and into the driver's seat locking both doors.

"Mr. Brownell . . ." Cyg yelled in the closed car. "I was not drinking . . . *Oooooo*, I hope Waldo makes a quarry out of his potato bed."

They shot backward out of the driveway almost giving Cyg whiplash.

When Aunt Lena waved and blew a kiss, Cyg poked out her tongue.

"That's no way to treat your lovely aunt," Darius pointed out, his voice mild.

"She's a Benedict Arnold in skirts." Cyg spat the words at him. "The two of you should start a kidnap for hire company. You'd be an instant success. Vipers."

"Tonight we are guests of honor at the party my aunt is hosting for us at the Gideon. Your folks will be here. I had my private jet pick them up."

"My father and mother will not be one whit impressed by that." Cyg sat rod straight in her seat, looking out the windshield.

"I intend to do everything I can to impress my future in-laws."

"Don't be a complacent ass," Cyg frothed.

"Complacent? With you as a wife? Don't be funny. I'll probably be old before my time. How many children should we have?"

"You are without doubt one of . . . What did you say?"

"I'd like three. A boy and two girls."

"No way." Cyg glared at him. "Two boys and one girl. And I won't change my mind." She lifted her chin.

"All right, darling. Whatever you say. See how easy it is to handle me. I'll be putty in your hands."

Cyg sat there, clenching and unclenching her hands and teeth.

"Remember your orthodontia," Darius said gently.

She inhaled deeply several times, picturing Darius on the rack and her hands turning the screws. The thought soothed her.

He patted her thigh. "We'll be happy. You'll see."

"Phil Tabor invited us to his house as . . . as call girls." She shoved the words out as though she was expelling garbage from her mouth.

"Phil has always had those kinds of parties. Even at Yale he always managed to have girls to rent for his friends."

Cyg flinched.

"Once," Darius kept speaking, "one of those girls punched him in the eye and told him what she thought of him. He wore an eye patch for an entire semester." He shot a quick look at her. "I have been around a good many years and been to many types of parties. I've met a variety of women—"

"I'll bet," Cyg said grimly.

"—handled business transactions in the maxi-millions, have dealt with integrity and with the very unscrupulous. I know gold from dross, my love. One look at you, with no words spoken, and

I knew that I wanted to love you. When I loved you I wanted you for my wife."

"Will your mother and father be there tonight?" Cyg sagged into the leather seat.

"Maybe. They both have had several marriages apiece, but they might be there. They have nothing to do with my life, and I really have nothing to do with theirs. I'm not like them. And though I have been divorced, my marriage with you is for a lifetime. I want us to have a family. Christmases together . . . Thanksgiving . . . Fourth of July . . ."

"Arbor Day." Cyg felt hope curl inside her.

"That too, crazy lady."

Cyg's head swiveled toward him, her eyes loving the look of those long fingers curved around the wheel. "What if I want to work after we're married?"

He threw her a quick glance. "Do you want to live here in Saratoga and be a physiotherapist?"

"Masseuse. I like it, but I could give it up."

"Would you like a job with the firm? Name it. You're the boss's wife and once we're married, you'll have fifty percent of the voting shares."

"No!"

"Yes. Everything that I have will belong to you, my love, including my life. Will you keep me?"

"A month or two, anyway." Cyg tried to smile. "Darius, I don't want money or things. I can't be part owner of your firm."

"Too late. The papers are already drawn. Cygnet Melton Chadwick, very rich lady."

"Oh, Lord."

Ten

Cyg was overjoyed to see her parents that evening when she and Darius went to the Gideon for the party Maura and Lena were cohosting for them.

"Dear child, Lena told me that I would love the man you'd chosen and I do. He's perfect for you." Her mother beamed at her, then reached out a hand to Darius who stood close to Cyg. He took her mother's hand. "I can see that you love her."

"Very much . . . from the moment I first saw her across a room full of people." Darius looked down at Cyg, not trying to hide his feelings. "But it took twenty-four hours to realize it was love."

Cyg's father shook hands with Darius, assessing the younger man with a long, cool stare. "I hope you'll make her happy."

"Every day she lives," Darius promised.

"Talk's cheap." Mr. Melton's five-foot-nine inches challenged Darius.

"Sir, I will never knowingly hurt Cygnet . . . by word or action. I'm sure we'll disagree on many things . . ."

"True." Cyg snuggled closer to him, the champagne silk gown she was wearing rustling round Darius's pant leg. She felt his arm tighten as she leaned on him.

His quick smile her way sobered as he looked at her father. "But even with that, I will make every effort to spare her pain. My word in business is considered gold, sir, I give you my word on this, the most important thing in my life, our marriage."

Cyg's father looked from Darius to Cyg and back again, then nodded. "I'll give you fifty years with her . . . if it hasn't worked in that time, I'll take her back."

Darius grinned like a boy as he pumped his future father-in-law's hand. "Fair enough."

"Now may I dance with my daughter, Darius?"

Cyg was delighted at Darius's reluctance to give her up even to her own father. She couldn't resist reaching up to give her fiancé a kiss on the mouth before she was swung away in her father's arms.

Darius stood there watching her, his feelings exposed for all to see. His Aunt Maura had to pull on his arm twice before he would look her way and be introduced to the people she had beside her.

"Your mother almost fainted when Maura informed her that the president had called to convey his regrets and that his wife had sent a Steuben glass vase with their best wishes." Her father chuckled.

Cyg looked at her parent with loving amusement. "And I suppose you just shrugged and acted unimpressed?"

"She and Lena were ready to kill me." He stared into her face, having to look up at his tall slim daughter. "I like Maura Tiebold. She is a very plain woman . . . and her nephew loves you."

Cyg nodded. "It was like lightning striking." She sighed, sighting Darius at once in the crowd of people. They smiled at one another. "I didn't believe you, when you told me that about you and mother: How you knew at once that it was forever." She looked over her father's shoulder at Darius, who was talking to her mother but still managed to look at her much of the time. "With Darius, it was like the missing puzzle pieces of my life fitting together. It was so fast, so beautiful, so lovely."

"William Butler Yeats said it best when he wrote the poem 'Never Give All the Heart.' "

"Beautiful, father." Cyg felt a sting of moisture in her eyes. "Because that's exactly what I thought of . . . that poem."

The two days left until the wedding flew by with the three older women reveling in all the confusion. Cyg felt like an automaton. Her dress designed by Charine of New York was ecru silk that enhanced her deep blond hair and her honey-colored eyes. The Victorian style with the high ruched neck in silk and the train caught in the back with a bustle made her tall slender figure classic and quite beautiful. Her hair was caught at the crown with a silk rose in the same material as the dress, her hair and veil cascading down her back in a fall. She wore the teardrop earrings that had belonged to Darius's grandmother and her engagement ring on her right hand. Maura Tiebold handed her a garter that had been hers and her mother's when she had married. The blue ribbons and hand-woven lace were interspersed with diamonds that winked in the warm light as Cyg pulled it up almost to her knee. Her shoes were medium-heeled handcrafted cream kid that matched the dress. She carried a tussie mussie as Maura called it, of tiny cream-colored roses with cream colored streamers that Darius had sent her.

Her mother was dressed in pale pink; Maura in pale green; Lena in beige. All the dresses were floor-length and designed by Charine for the occasion. Each of the women wore wrist corsages of complementing roses and carried clutch bags of the same material as the gowns. It was Cyg's wish that Maura and her aunt be her attendants and that both parents should give her away.

Her father looked distinguished in a morning suit with striped pants and long-tailed coat. "The only other time your mother and I had clothes designed just for us was when we went to the Owners' Convention in Atlanta. Then we had Max Schwarz make us suits. We still wear them." He looked down at himself in the morning suit and chuckled. "Course I don't know when I'll wear this again."

"You look wonderful, father."

"So do you, my darling child. I am so happy for you. Come along now. We are all going in the Rolls. Darius will meet us at the church. He made me promise that I would keep my eye on you or he wouldn't have allowed you to spend last night here at Lena's."

"Bossy man," Cyg breathed, turning to greet her mother and aunt as they came into the bedroom.

"No, no crying you two," Cyg's father admonished as his wife took out her hankie.

"Of course, we won't cry." Aunt Lena cleared her throat as she edged the veil down over Cyg's face, then stepped back.

The four stared at one another for a moment, then her father coughed and said it was time to go.

Maura was sitting in the back of the Rolls fidgeting so much that Lena had to laugh. "You're not the one getting married, Maura Tiebold," Aunt Lena chortled.

"I was less nervous then." Maura sighed, making Mr. Melton, who was sitting sitting next to the driver, turn around and laugh.

"Now don't start that or Muriel will be having fits."

Cyg's mother glared at her husband. "Just you make sure you don't trip."

Cyg listened to their words and smiled, but her thoughts had flown on to the church. Darius, Darius, Darius. He was waiting for her.

When she stepped out of the car in front of the church, she took little note of the people there.

She listened to the chiming of the carillon, then she was inside. Someone was straightening her veil, then her train. Her father spoke to her, she placed her hand on his arm, her mother coming to her other side. As if in a dream, she watched Maura and Lena precede her, side by side, then she was moving forward, amazed at the crowd of people turning to watch her progress down the long aisle. She looked up and forgot the people. She forgot her mother and father, even the minister who stood there in white, a prayer book open in his hands. Darius was smiling at her and moving to meet her.

"Dearly beloved . . ."

The words echoed out into the cavern of prayer, the vows lifting into the air as though for a blessing.

Cyg heard her own tremulous responses as though she were a witness and not a participant. Darius spoke his vows in a deep resonant voice that carried up, up high into the Gothic structure.

When they turned to face the crowd, Cygnet paused and looked at Darius. He inclined his head toward her, one eyebrow raised in question. "You're mine now. You're my husband." Her calm statement penetrated the rising chords of the Recessional.

"Yes, Mrs. Chadwick, I'm yours." Darius's voice was hoarse, a muscle jumped along his cheekbone.

The reception at the Gideon was mass confusion for Cyg, but she didn't feel threatened by it. Darius was close to her, his palm warm on her back, his breath often feathering her face as he bent over her.

When Phil Tabor approached along the receiving line, Cyg looked at him with cool detachment. He leaned over to kiss her and she leaned back, one hand coming up to push at him gently. "Go away," she whispered, a smile on her face. "You annoy me."

Phil's smile collapsed, his eyes shooting left and right, his hand dropping to his side.

Cyg leaned forward just a bit. "And don't bother approaching us on any business deals anymore. We aren't interested."

Darius turned from the person he was greeting, just catching her last words. He gazed narrow eyed at Phil. "You heard my partner, Phil." He folded his hands in front of him until Phil Tabor moved away. Then he smiled at his wife. "Did I tell you that you look beautiful today?"

"Only three hundred times. More, I want more." Cyg dimpled at him, feeling like a melted marshmallow inside.

"Oh, you will definitely get more, Mrs. Chadwick. Much, much more." Darius grinned. "You're blushing, love. I like that."

"Fools blush." She turned away to speak to a guest, feeling his fingers kneading her waist.

"How far down does your blush go?" Darius whispered into her hair. "And is your garter fastened high on your thigh?"

"Monster. Stop it." Cyg felt heat up and down her legs.

When they sat down to eat, Cyg stared at the people out in front of her. "Darius, isn't that . . . ?" she mumbled into her plate.

"Yes, he's on the Supreme Court. And there's the senator. You met them all in the receiving line." Darius fed her some cake.

"How is it that you know so many show business people?" Cyg sipped her champagne.

"Oh, didn't I mention that we own a TV network?"

"Never mind, don't tell me any more." Cyg glared at him when he laughed. "Tell me about our honeymoon."

"No, it's a surprise."

Cyg tried to wheedle it out of him while they danced. She tried to cajole when they were changing for the trip to the airport. She threatened that she would have a tantrum at Kennedy Airport when they landed. Darius just kissed the tip of her nose.

She had expected to take a commercial jet when they were at Kennedy. It shocked her when another plane belonging to Chadwick Industries was waiting for them.

"But Darius, you must tell me now." She sat on his lap, cuddled to his chest as they flew out over the Atlantic.

"Bermuda, my darling. I have a friend, Aaron Lathrop, who is letting me have his villa for a month. If you like it there, we'll see about getting our own place."

"Bermuda! We'll swim and sail and—"

"And be alone," Darius finished. "It's very hot there at this time of year, but the house is air conditioned. Best of all, we can be completely alone."

"Nice. I'll get a tan."

"Probably not." Darius chuckled.

"Sex fiend."

"Yes."

"Good," answered Mrs. Chadwick, nibbling at her husband's ear.

When the plane landed, they were still holding each other. Darius leaned back to look at her. "I hope our children never find out how much their father likes to cuddle with their mother."

"I'll tell them."

"Don't you dare." Darius shook her gently.

"I will unless you promise to give me what I want."

"Name it."

"You." She leaned back this time to look at him. "Easy, huh?"

"You told me that before." His voice was husky.

Cyg was lifted off his lap as the plane taxied to a stop in the beautiful turquoise-and-white atmosphere that was Bermuda. "I want you to remember that. If we lost all our money tomorrow that is still all that I would want, but . . ."

They were interrupted by an attendant who knocked at the door of their compartment, then entered to announce it was time for them to go through Customs.

Throngs filled the area waiting to begin their stay in Bermuda.

When they stepped outside to get into the waiting car, Cyg staggered at the heat.

"Maybe I shouldn't have brought you here at this time of year, but I wanted to be alone with you . . . and fast," Darius muttered as the air-conditioned car cocooned them.

"I need to talk to you, as well." Cyg leaned against him.

"I know. Didn't you know that I could read your mind by now?"

"I think it's more than that." Cyg looked up at him feeling very serious. "I think you can feel what I'm going to say before I say it."

"You do the same with me. We're part of each other."

"Yes, but . . ."

The car whirled around the curves across the narrow causeway and up and across the island. For a moment the two of them were distracted by the beauty of their surroundings, pointing out to each other the wonders of the Jewel of the Atlantic.

"Who is Aaron Lathrop?" Cyg asked, her head swiveling right, so as not to miss any of the lovely houses, that looked like pastel frosted bonbons scattered on the hillsides.

"A business associate whose firm has done most of the construction work for our firm, and who has become a personal friend over the years. You'll meet him, his wife, and four children one day."

"Four children? Are they older?" Cyg turned back to look at Darius.

"Not really. The first three are Oriental children

that they adopted, the last is their natural child. After you're with them for a time, you can't tell which child is Oriental." Darius shook his head and laughed at her disbelieving hoot. "It's true. Those kids are so much alike . . . inside, that is, that they seem to disappear into one another. Wonderful family." Darius smiled as though some small remembrance warmed him.

"I look forward to meeting them," Cyg said, wanting to get to know people who had such an emotional pull on Darius.

"But not for a while." Darius reached out for her, tugging her close to him, just as the car made a sharp turn and plowed up the crushed stone drive.

"Windrift," Cyg whispered, reading the sign. Then she forgot what she was going to say when she saw the house. "Beautiful."

Darius introduced Lazslo who took charge of the luggage and told them when dinner would be, then disappeared. Darius turned to look at her as Cyg twirled around the airy bedroom. "Like it, Mrs. Chadwick?"

"Yes." Cyg whirled right into his arms.

Darius folded her close, his mouth running over her face and down her neck. "Alone. Finally alone. We're going to talk and make love, make love and talk. By the time we are ready to go back to the mainland, you will know how much I love you, Mrs. Chadwick."

"Darius . . ." Cyg gulped, feeling her eyes sting. "Don't say any more until I tell you about . . . about Phil Tabor."

"There's no need. I know all about you, my love."

"Darius, you said, the evening of our party at the Gideon that it looked as though I handled Phil by myself . . . and I had. I poured my champagne down the front of him."

"I know that. We talked about it that night." Darius was patient, his one hand caressing her from thigh to breast.

"But, don't you see, Phil talked to others about me . . . and they will talk to more. It could be an endless chain of embarrassment for you, Darius. Wherever we went, there could be whisperings." Cyg could feel the muscles in her face knot and stretch over her bones.

Darius looked down at her, an exasperated amusement on his face. "Don't you listen, woman of mine. The only people who would give credence to something Phil said are people like him . . . people of no account. Even his brother considers Phil a loser. It was only out of loyalty to Fred Tabor that I was at Phil's house that weekend . . . for which I will always give thanks." Darius cupped her face between his hands, lowering himself closer to her. "I knew when we were together two days that you *were*—the lady I had been searching for my whole life." He bent and lifted her into his arms, carrying her to the bed. He sat down with her on his lap. "I also knew that you didn't frequent parties like that, love . . . if it's important for you to hear that." He lay back against the pillows stacked near the headboard of the bed. "But you see, even if you were a call girl—and I would have been able to tell, darling—then I would have still wanted you. I wanted you and loved you from the moment you trailed in that door after Phil and Kim." His hands ran up and down her back soothing her. "I'll want you like that when we're in our hundreds." He looked down at her, the fire in his eyes melting her, shaping her, honing her just for him. "I want you to be the mother of my children and the love of my life for all time. Will you be my mistress, my lover, my girl friend, my lady, my woman?"

"I . . . I love you, Darius, and I want to be all to you, if you promise one thing."

"You can have anything but a divorce or separation." Darius nuzzled her cheek.

"Promise me you'll outlive me," Cyg whispered.

The silence in the room lengthened so that the ocean song sounded no longer muted by air conditioning, the breeze off the Atlantic ruffling the palms.

"Wife of mine, you ask a great deal, but I will do my best to live with you all your years." Darius sounded the words like a vow, making Cyg sigh with relief.

She leaned up from his chest, studying the lazy, possessive look of him as he sprawled against the bank of pillows on the king-sized bed. "I am going to make love to you, Mr. Chadwick," she pronounced, feeling a love power course through her veins like hot steel. "Don't be scared."

Darius's lazy look sharpened into a sensual smile that enveloped her like velvet. "I'll try to control my fear." His teeth snapped together ever so gently, their whiteness widening in a soft snarl.

Cyg leaned over him, her fingers finding every pore in that close-shaven face as they explored down his neck to his tie, which she loosened, the buttons on his shirt that she pulled apart. She paused for a moment, then she bent to nibble on his jawline. "You taste good, husband."

"Do I?" Darius laughed, almost masking the tremor in his voice.

Cyg loved knowing that he was in thrall to her. "Yes." Her teeth nipped at his ear, making his body tremble.

"Lady . . ." Darius inhaled, his hands coming up to clutch at her waist.

"No—" Cyg loosened his fingers, pushing his hands back to his sides. "Not your turn yet," she whispered, her mouth running down his chest, loving the feel of the curling hair on her lips.

"Cygnet." Darius groaned as she pulled his arms from the sleeves of his shirt and kissed each shoulder.

"Yes, dear," she crooned, unfastening his belt,

then getting him to lift his hips so that she might help him shed his trousers. "Isn't this fun?"

"Fun is not the word I would have chosen." Darius reached for her, then frowned when she held up both hands to forestall him.

"Not yet, love." She knelt in front of him, loosening the blouse of her suit, casting it on the floor, her skirt and slip following. She sat back and rolled her stockings down her leg one by one, all the time smiling at her husband who stared at her in rapt concentration.

When she leaned over him in just bra and briefs she felt dazed at the love emanating from him. "I do love you very, very much husband."

"The feeling is mutual, Cygnet." Darius reached for her and this time he would not be denied. He swung her under him, then slowly unhooked the front fastening of her bra. "About you breast feeding our two boys and a girl."

"Two girls and a boy . . . and I won't change my mind." Cyg held his head tight to her breast as his mouth closed over one nipple and teased and caressed it.

"Whatever." Darius's voice was husky. "I'm not sure I'll allow you to do that. I don't think I can share you even with our children."

"We'll worry about that when the time comes." Cyg gasped, feeling his mouth move down her body.

"In the meantime, I'll practice."

"Do that." Cyg squeaked, feeling his mouth give her the most intimate of caresses, her body arching in response. "Darius!"

"Yes, darling," he crooned, answering her at once with his body as he lifted over her.

Their joining was one kaleidoscopic explosion of giving as each tried to satisfy the other with more and more love.

Cyg lay trembling in his arms, her hands sliding down his perspiring body. "That was so wonderful. Should we market it for mankind?"

"What? And wipe out wars and pestilence and all that good stuff?" Darius mumbled into her neck. "Good idea, but it won't work."

Cyg lifted her head. "Darius, what if I'm pregnant now?" She felt awed by the thought.

"Then you will probably delight the hell out of your parents and our aunts." He smiled at her.

She stared at him. "I was sorry your mother didn't get to the wedding."

He shrugged and smiled at her. "I truly didn't mind. I'm used to it." He kissed her nose. "I have you, love. I don't need anyone else."

"Your father is . . . unusual." Cyg picked at the hairs on his chest.

"Make a pass at you?" Darius chuckled at her look of surprise. "Why didn't you upend an ice bucket on his head? If his sister Maura had caught him, she would have. She dislikes her brother intensely." Darius was very matter of fact, his eyes serene. "I don't hate either one of them. I guess I just feel sorry for my parents. It's been years since I've had any desire to spend time with them." He touched her face with one finger. "But if the time ever comes when they need me . . ."

"I know you'll be there for them, Darius Chadwick. *You* don't have to tell me that."

"Now tell me what my father, the roué, said to you."

Cyg grimaced at him. "He asked me if we had lived together long enough to know our own minds. He also told me that if I ever found myself bored with you . . . to call . . ." Cyg faltered at the furious expression building on Darius's face. "You said you were used to them . . ."

"I am also damn jealous of you," he thundered, making his chest heave under Cyg's form. "The old fool . . . I might have thrown him through a window," Darius barked. "It's nothing to laugh at." He glowered at her, but Cyg couldn't stop laughing as she lay on his chest.

"Can't you see Aunt Lena and Aunt Maura standing there openmouthed while you threw your father through one of the windows at the Gideon?"

Darius's chest rumbled with laughter. "Your mother would have put her hand to her cheek and looked the other way."

"You are a nasty man." Cyg pummeled his body. "Thinking of starting a riot at my wedding reception."

"Ummmm, I love it when you do that," Darius growled in her ear. "Makes the cave man come out in me."

"Me Jane, you Tarzan." Cyg thumped her breast.

"Don't do that." He held her hands away from her body and kissed her breasts, first one, then the other, his mouth lingering. "I don't want bruises on this body . . . not ever."

"Yes, sir." She sighed. "Darius, we can't stay here all day. What will Lazslo think?"

"If I know Aaron Lathrop, and I do, I'll bet he spends a great deal of time in bed with that gorgeous wife of his."

"Gorgeous, is she?" Cyg threw herself at him, almost tumbling them both off the bed as she tried to give him a good thumping. Laughing, they held each other, their faces close, noses touching. "I have never, never had so much fun, felt so . . . so relaxed," Cyg cooed.

"You mean it's better than the Roosevelt Baths? The massage?"

Cyg sighed. "I've only had two massages and baths. Never had the time for another . . ."

Darius flipped off the bed and strode to the bathroom.

Cyg watched him, mouth agape as he came back into the bedroom with ointment, towels, and a determined grin on his face. "You don't know how to do it."

"I've had plenty of massages in my time, woman.

I think I can give you a fair one. Turn on your tummy."

"We'll get ointment on the sheets," Cyg muttered, her body front down. When there was silence from Darius, she looked around at him.

He was staring down at her body, his eyes fixed and glittering. "You're so beautiful." One hand reached down to touch her back. "You have the roundest bottom. I love it."

"Darius . . ." she giggled, ". . . you would be fired the first day as a masseur."

"I think I'll have them painted," he mused, sitting on the side of the bed and opening the ointment.

Cyg jackknifed around to face him. "Paint what? My backside? Darius Chadwick, you . . . you . . ." Cyg sputtered, shoving at him.

He frowned at her, a hurt look on his face. "Anger? Just because a man wants to paint his wife's best side . . . ouch, that hurts, no . . . don't tickle . . . not nice . . ." He caught her to him, laughing. "I love it when you lose your temper."

"I haven't yet you . . . you . . ." Cyg took hold of his ears and pulled him down to her, giving him a kiss. "How am I going to control you?"

"Easy. Just say 'Darius, time for bed.' I'll come running like a lap dog," he assured her.

Cyg felt the smile leave her face. "When I think how it was with us when we met the first time, I recall a line from a poem by William Butler Yeats."

Darius seemed to sense her emotion. "What was it, love?"

"The quotation goes . . . 'For everything that's lovely is but a brief, dreamy kind of delight.' Nice, huh?"

"Perfect. Except ours is going to be an *eternal* delight, my own love." Darius gave her a soft, searching kiss.

THE EDITOR'S CORNER

Bantam is blessed with the best sales force in the publishing business. Of course this is biased coming from me, but I think a lot of folks out there would confirm the truth of this statement. Why mention the sales force? Because they're unheralded . . . and very important. They are the men and women who make it easy for you to get our books each and every month in every part of the country. And to all the members of that field sales force we in the home office and the *LOVESWEPT* authors, want to express our gratitude . . . gratitude. There's a proverb that says: "Gratitude is the heart's memory." We couldn't express our feelings better than that proverb does. Thanks, Bantam sales force. You kept the faith! You did the job!

And have we got love stories for you readers next month! Here she comes again, friends! Funny, delightful, Billie Green with another charmer . . . **A VERY RELUCTANT KNIGHT** (#16). Heroine Maggie Sims just knew wealthy, irresistibly handsome Mark Wilding was all wrong for her in every way—for example, far too tall for her five-foot-zero frame. "So I'll slump," he drawled. "But you're name brand and I'm generic," she countered. "Maggie, Maggie." He laughed. "I may be name brand, but I defy anyone to label you. You, love, are strictly one of a kind . . . which is why I don't intend to let you disappear out of my life." A tornado had brought them together in a storm cellar, but it was mild compared to the stormy relationship that followed.

(continued)

Remember in last month's editor's corner that I teased you about reading STORMY VOWS very carefully. I hope you've done it . . . if not, go back and take a special look at that tall, dark, and dreamy director, Jake Dominic. Jake is the hero of Iris Johansen's next romance . . . **TEMPEST AT SEA** (#17). From the moment Jake collides with Jane Smith, a spunky and adorable intruder on his yacht, there's trouble at sea! And what delicious trouble. You already know a good deal about Jake from STORMY VOWS, so let me just tell you that Jane is more than his match. High-spirited, with a lively mind and a fresh loveliness, Jane draws Jake into a passionate net from which he's powerless to free himself! A delicious romp ensues! I promise you this is a fun-filled, unforgettable love story!

I'm *so* pleased to be able to introduce Sara Orwig as a LOVESWEPT author through her heartwarming, wonderfully believable romance **AUTUMN FLAMES** (#18). Heroine Lily Dunbar means to fire a warning shot to prevent a hunter from killing a rare animal, but instead her aim falters and she grazes the man himself. And the man is the formidable Chilean landholder, Reece Wakefield. But this mishap is just the beginning of Sara's truly charming story. And in addition to a love to remember, I bet you won't soon forget a one-eyed, feisty cat named General Jackson!

Your cards and letter inspire us; the way you've told us you've taken our romances into your hearts touches us. And with every degree of pride that each

LOVESWEPT author and editor experiences comes a renewed devotion to excellence in our romance publishing program!

Carolyn Nichols

Carolyn Nichols
  Editor
LOVESWEPT
Bantam Books, Inc.
666 Fifth Avenue
New York, NY 10103

Love Stories you'll never forget by authors you'll always remember

☐	21603	**Heaven's Price** #1 Sandra Brown	$1.95
☐	21604	**Surrender** #2 Helen Mittermeyer	$1.95
☐	21600	**The Joining Stone** #3 Noelle Berry McCue	$1.95
☐	21601	**Silver Miracles** #4 Fayrene Preston	$1.95
☐	21605	**Matching Wits** #5 Carla Neggers	$1.95
☐	21606	**A Love for All Time** #6 Dorothy Garlock	$1.95
☐	21607	**A Tryst With Mr. Lincoln?** #7 Billie Green	$1.95
☐	21602	**Temptation's Sting** #8 Helen Conrad	$1.95
☐	21608	**December 32nd . . . And Always** #9 Marie Michael	$1.95
☐	21609	**Hard Drivin' Man** #10 Nancy Carlson	$1.95
☐	21610	**Beloved Intruder** #11 Noelle Berry McCue	$1.95
☐	21611	**Hunter's Payne** #12 Joan J. Domning	$1.95
☐	21618	**Tiger Lady** #13 Joan Domning	$1.95
☐	21613	**Stormy Vows** #14 Iris Johansen	$1.95
☐	21614	**Brief Delight** #15 Helen Mittermeyer	$1.95

Buy them at your local bookstore or use this handy coupon for ordering:

Bantam Books, Inc., Dept. SW, 414 East Golf Road, Des Plaines, Ill. 60016

Please send me the books I have checked above. I am enclosing $_____ (please add $1.25 to cover postage and handling). Send check or money order—no cash or C.O.D.'s please.

Mr/Ms_____

Address_____

City/State_____ Zip_____

SW—8/83

Please allow four to six weeks for delivery. This offer expires 2/84.

SAVE $2.00 ON YOUR NEXT BOOK ORDER!
BANTAM BOOKS
Shop-at-Home Catalog

Now you can have a complete, up-to-date catalog of Bantam's inventory of over 1,600 titles—including hard-to-find books. And, you can save $2.00 on your next order by taking advantage of the money-saving coupon you'll find in this illustrated catalog. Choose from fiction and non-fiction titles, including mysteries, historical novels, westerns, cookbooks, romances, biographies, family living, health, and more. You'll find a description of most titles. Arranged by categoreis, the catalog makes it easy to find your favorite books and authors and to discover new ones.

So don't delay—send for this shop-at-home catalog and save money on your next book order.

Just send us your name and address and 50¢ to defray postage and handling costs.

BANTAM BOOKS, INC.
Dept. FC, 414 East Golf Road, Des Plaines, Ill. 60016

Mr./Mrs./Miss/Ms. _____
(please print)

Address _____

City _____ State _____ Zip _____

Do you know someone who enjoys books? Just give us their names and addresses and we'll send them a catalog too at no extra cost!

Mr./Mrs./Miss/Ms. _____

Address _____

City _____ State _____ Zip _____

Mr./Mrs./Miss/Ms. _____

Address _____

City _____ State _____ Zip _____

FC—2/83A